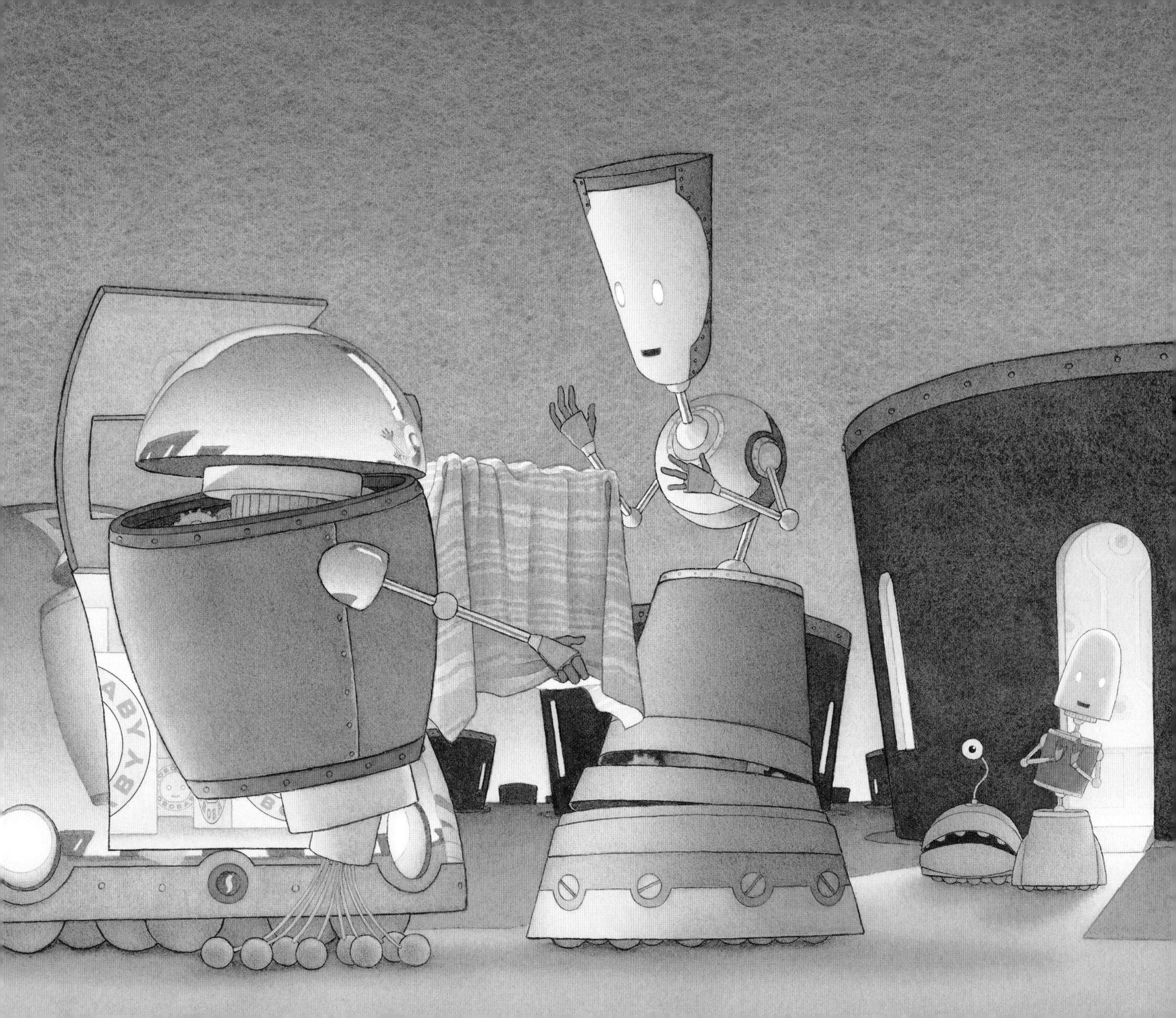

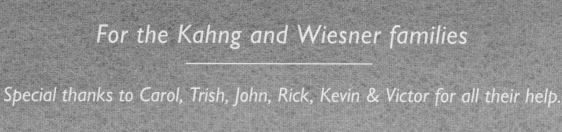

For the Kahng and Wiesner families

Special thanks to Carol, Trish, John, Rick, Kevin & Victor for all their help.

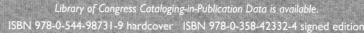

Clarion Books is an imprint of Houghton Mifflin Harcourt Publishing Company.
hmhbooks.com

The illustrations in this book were created in watercolor. The text was set in Gill Sans Semibold.
Book design by Carol Goldenberg • Lettering by John Green

Library of Congress Cataloging-in-Publication Data is available.
ISBN 978-0-544-98731-9 hardcover   ISBN 978-0-358-42332-4 signed edition

Manufactured in China
SCP 10 9 8 7 6 5 4 3 2
4500812482

ROBOBABY

DAVID WIESNER

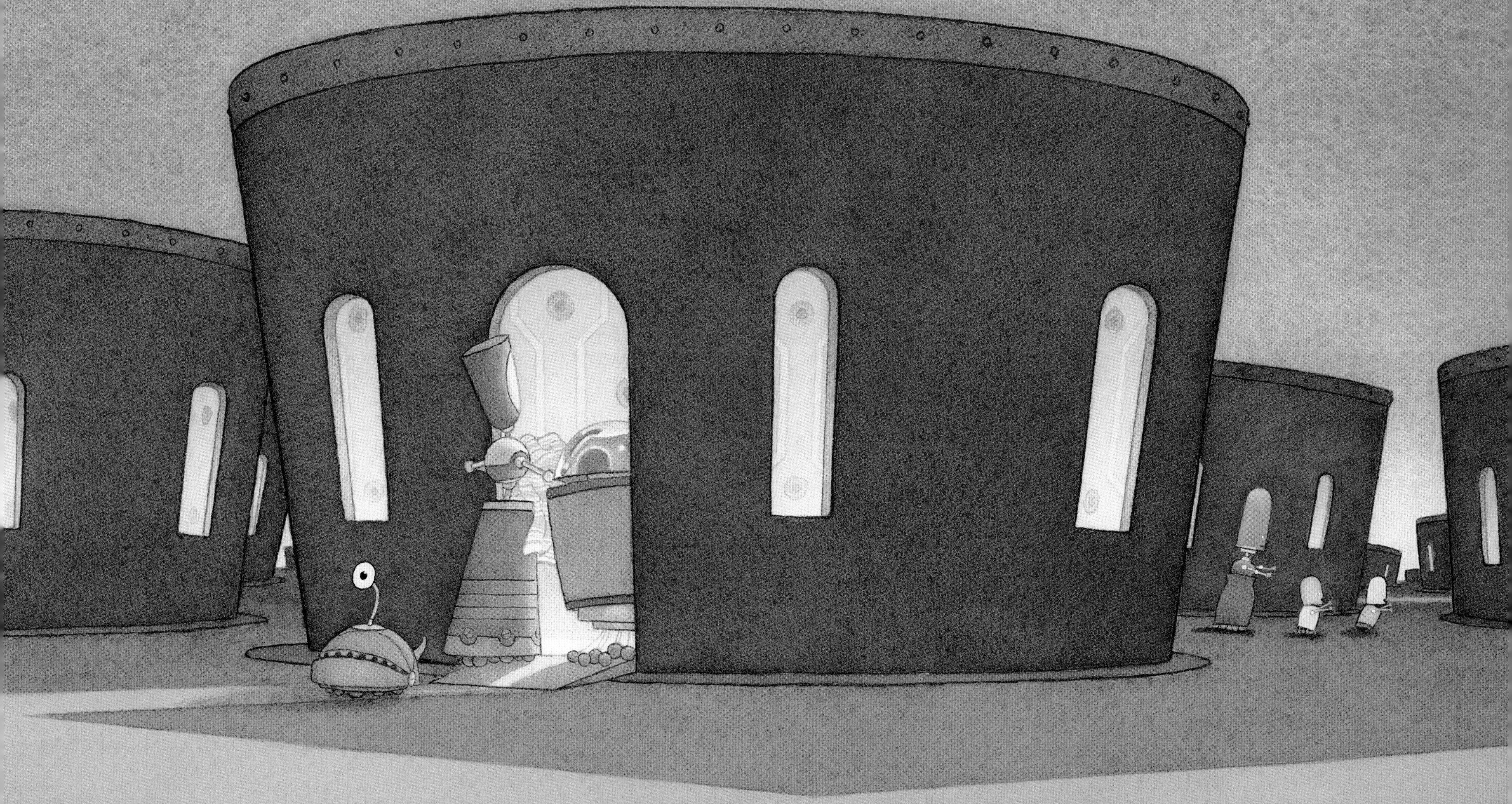

Clarion Books / Houghton Mifflin Harcourt / Boston • New York

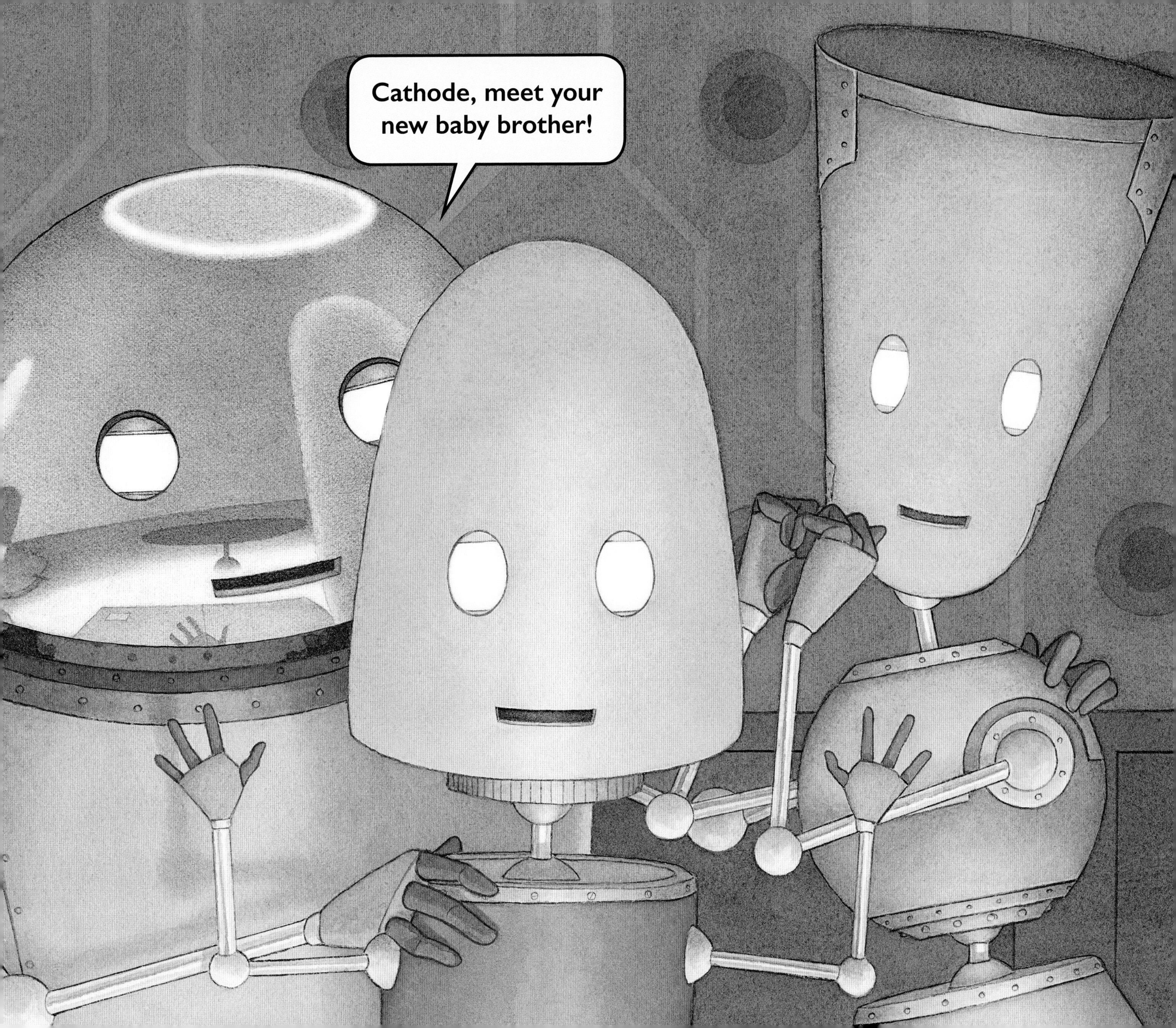
Cathode, meet your new baby brother!

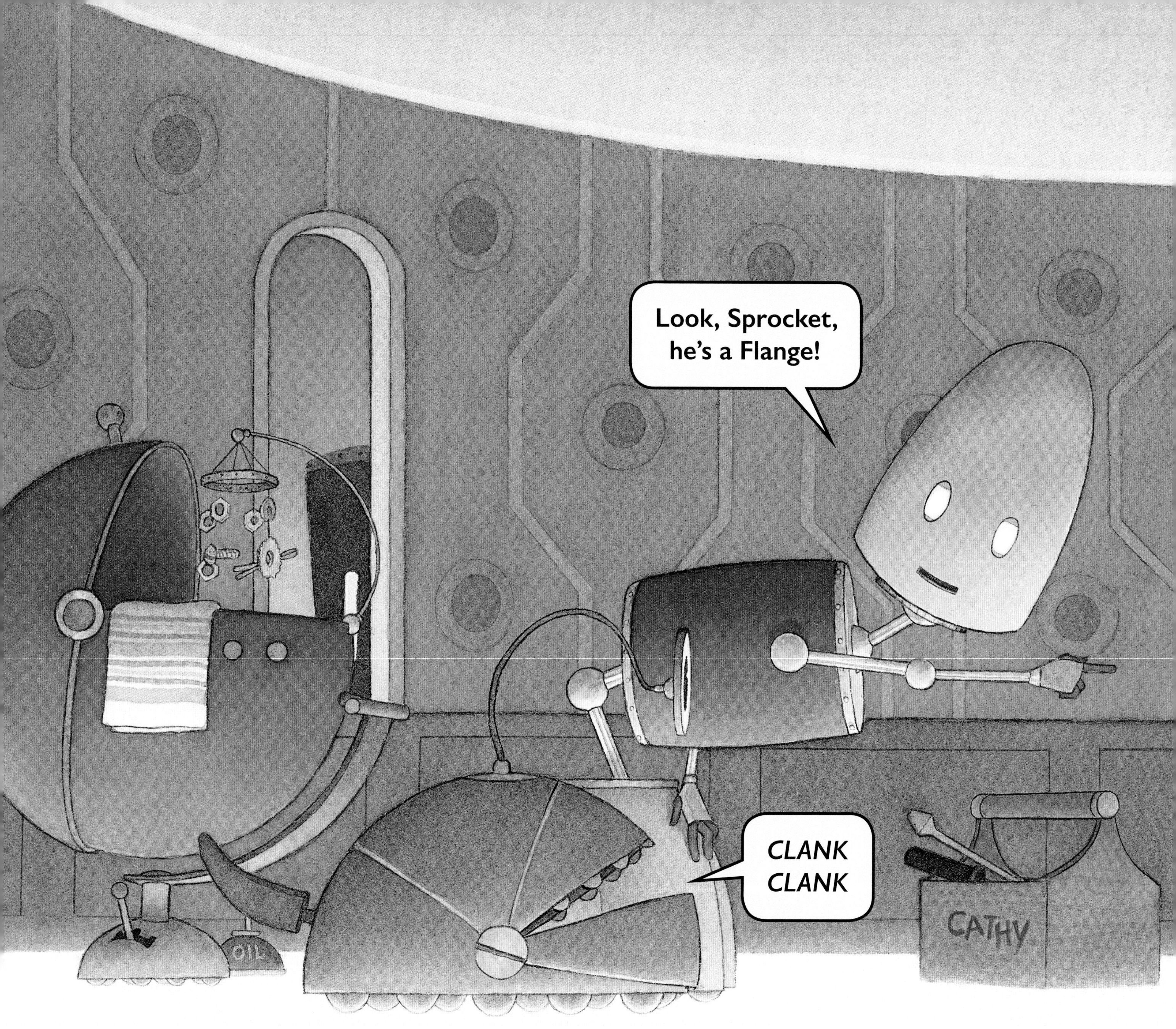
Look, Sprocket, he's a Flange!
CLANK CLANK
CATHY
OIL

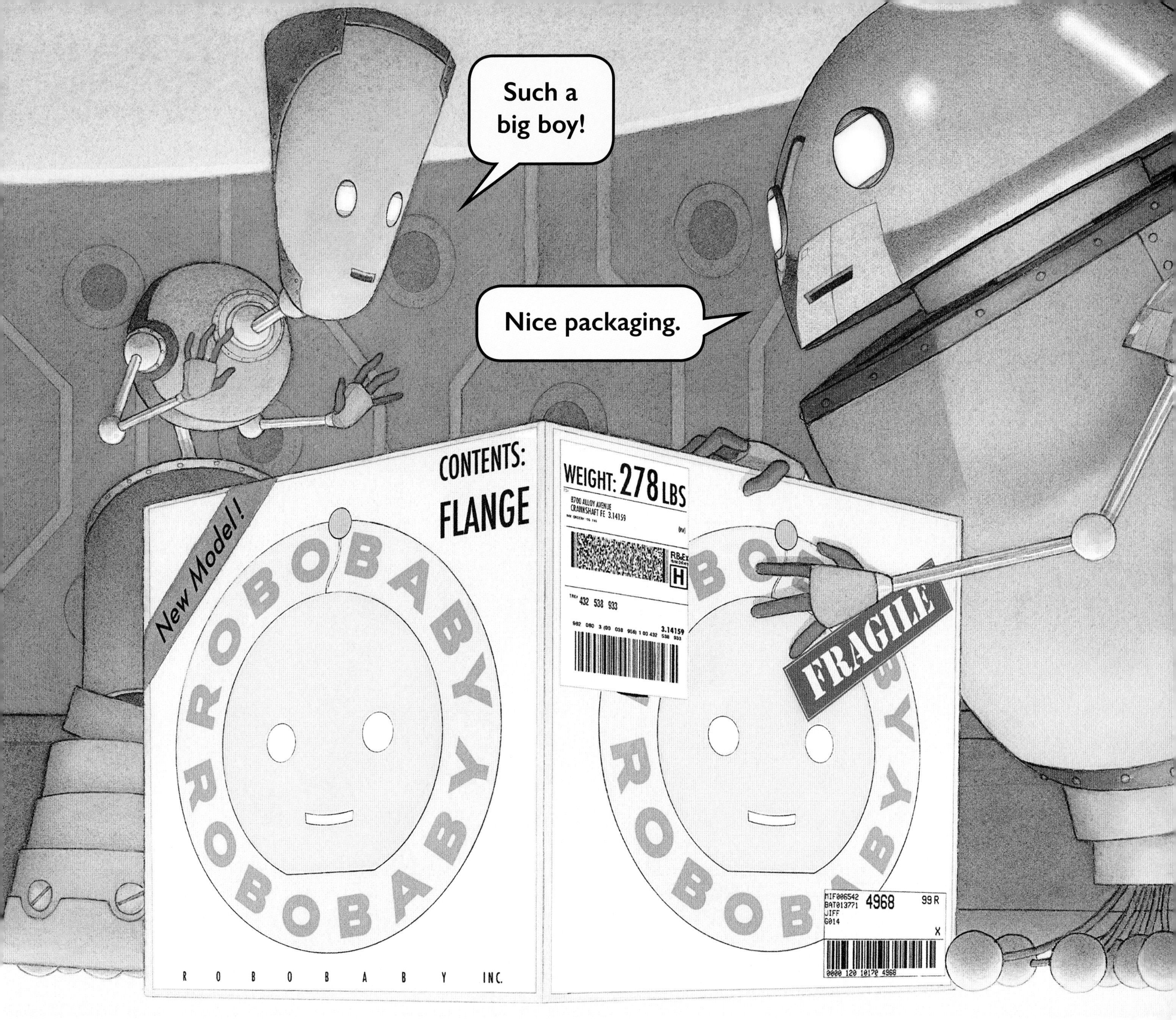
Such a big boy!
Nice packaging.
CONTENTS:
FLANGE
New Model!
ROBOBABY
WEIGHT: 278 LBS
8700 ALLOY AVENUE
CRANKSHAFT FE 3.14159
FRAGILE
R O B O B A B Y INC.

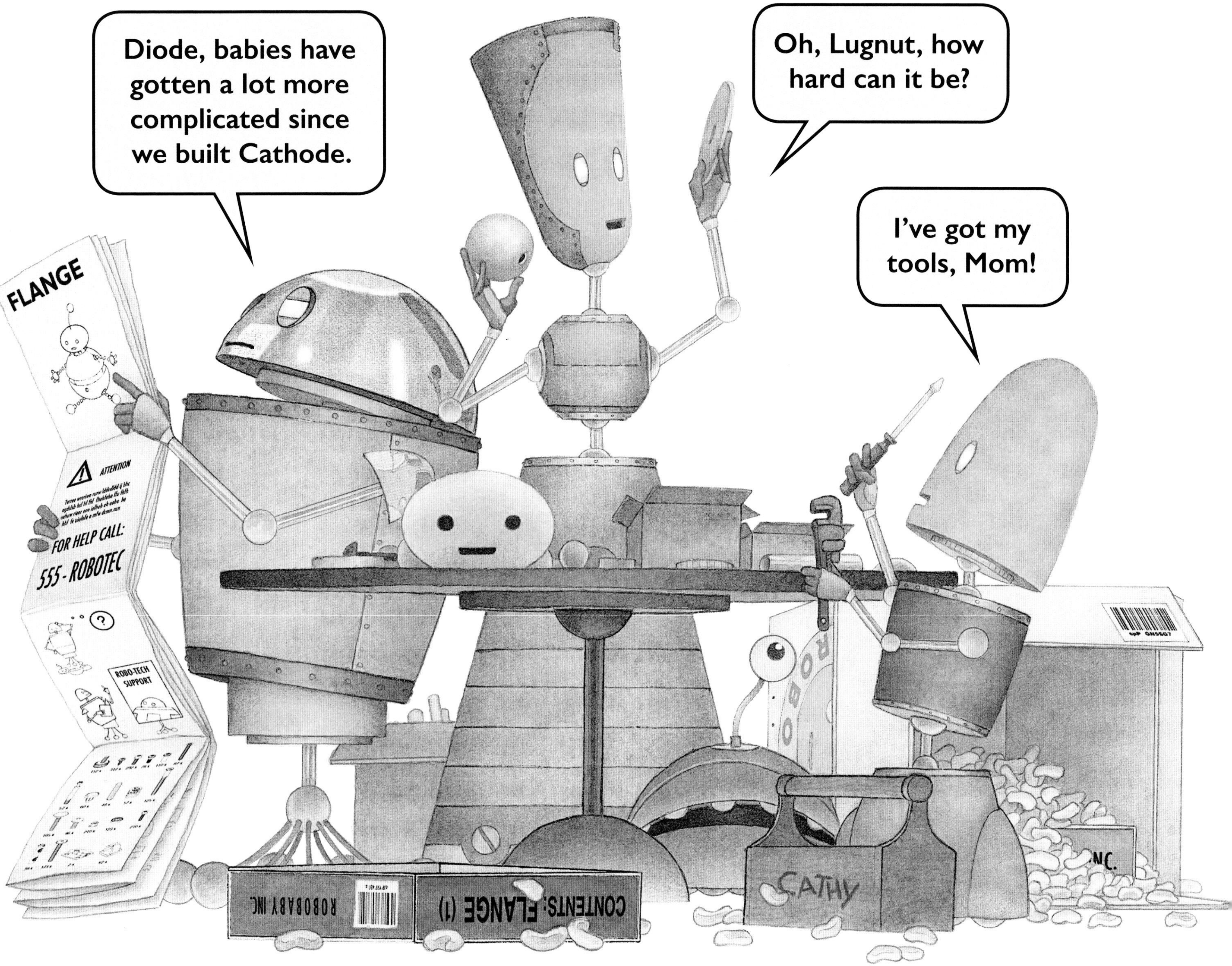
Diode, babies have gotten a lot more complicated since we built Cathode.
Oh, Lugnut, how hard can it be?
I've got my tools, Mom!
FLANGE
ATTENTION
FOR HELP CALL:
555-ROBOTEC
ROBO-TECH SUPPORT
CATHY
ROBOBABY INC
CONTENTS: FLANGE (1)

Thanks, Cathy…
…but this is a mother's job.
Easy!

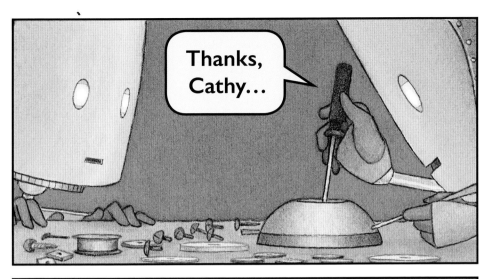

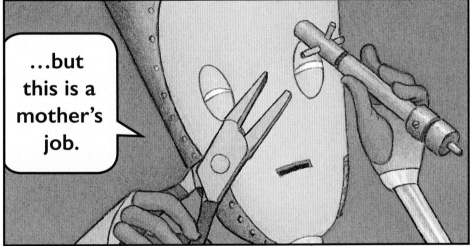

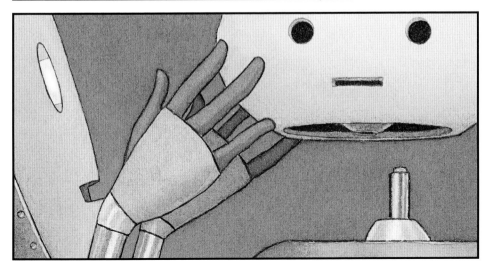

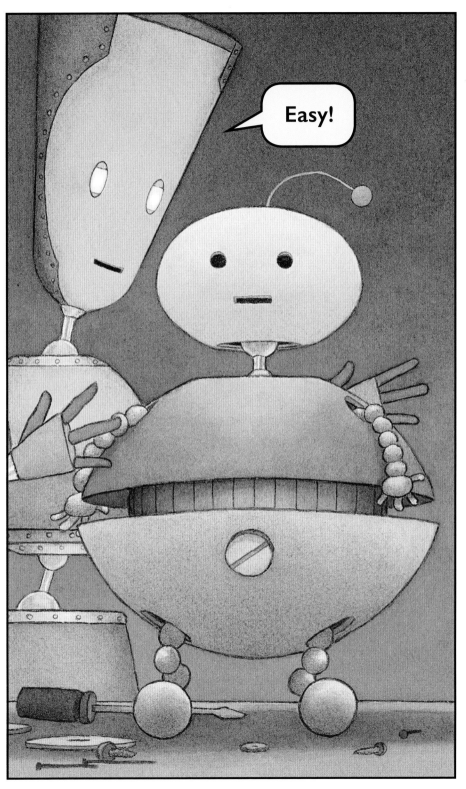

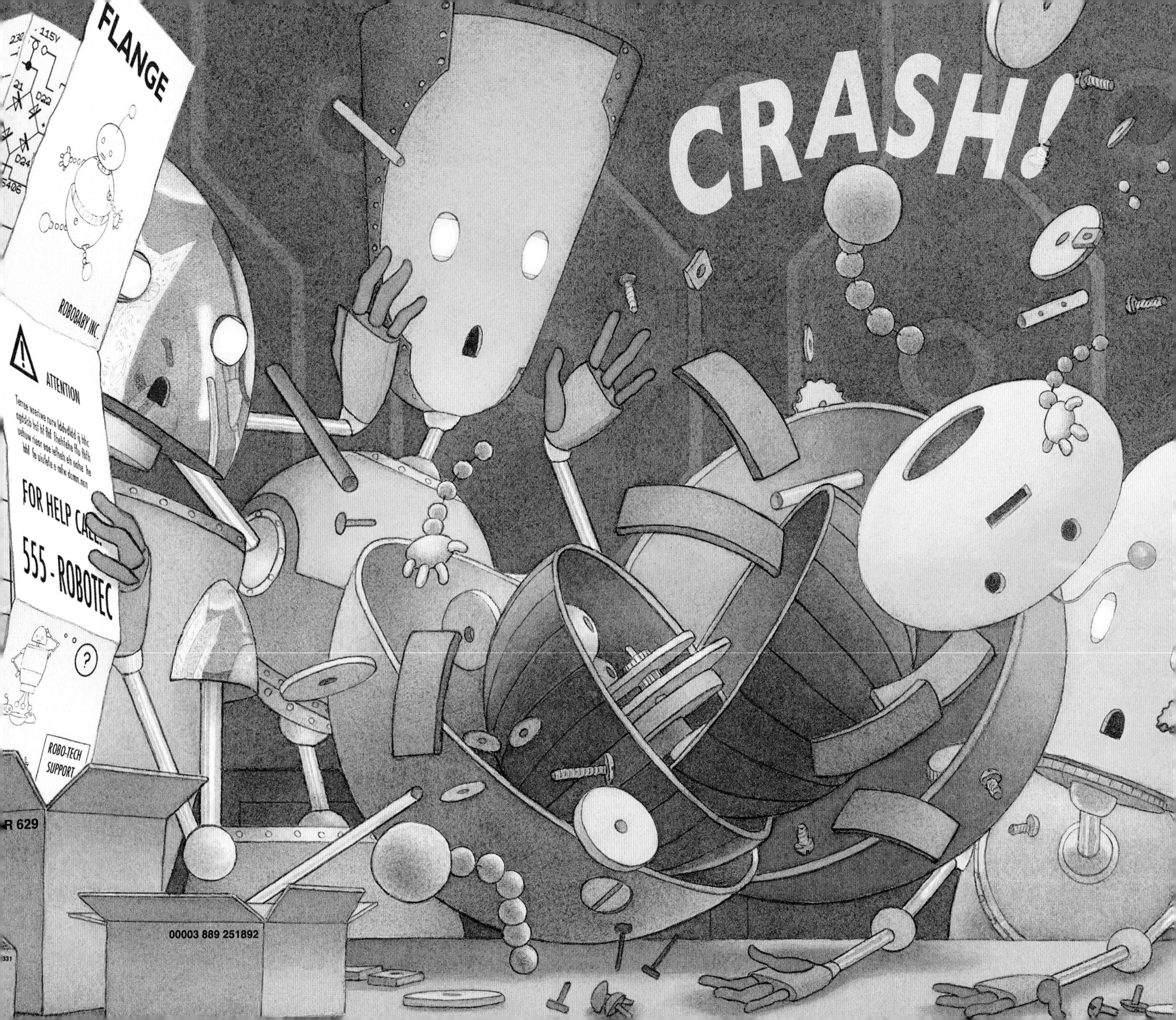
CRASH!
FLANGE
ROBOBABY INC.
ATTENTION
FOR HELP CALL:
555 - ROBOTEC
ROBO-TECH SUPPORT
R 629
00003 889 251892

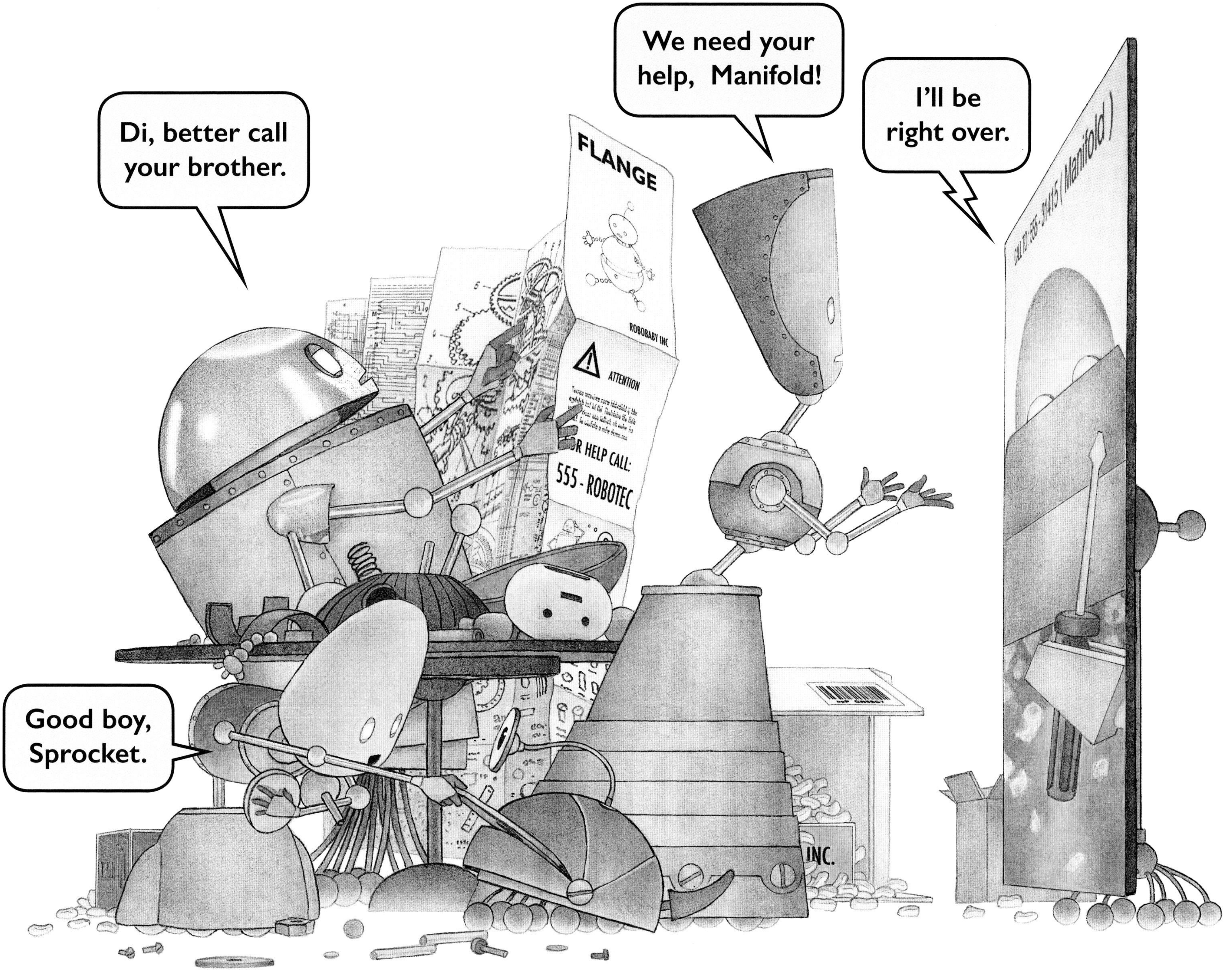

Di, better call your brother.
We need your help, Manifold!
I'll be right over.
Good boy, Sprocket.
FLANGE
ROBOBABY INC
ATTENTION
555 - ROBOTEC
INC.

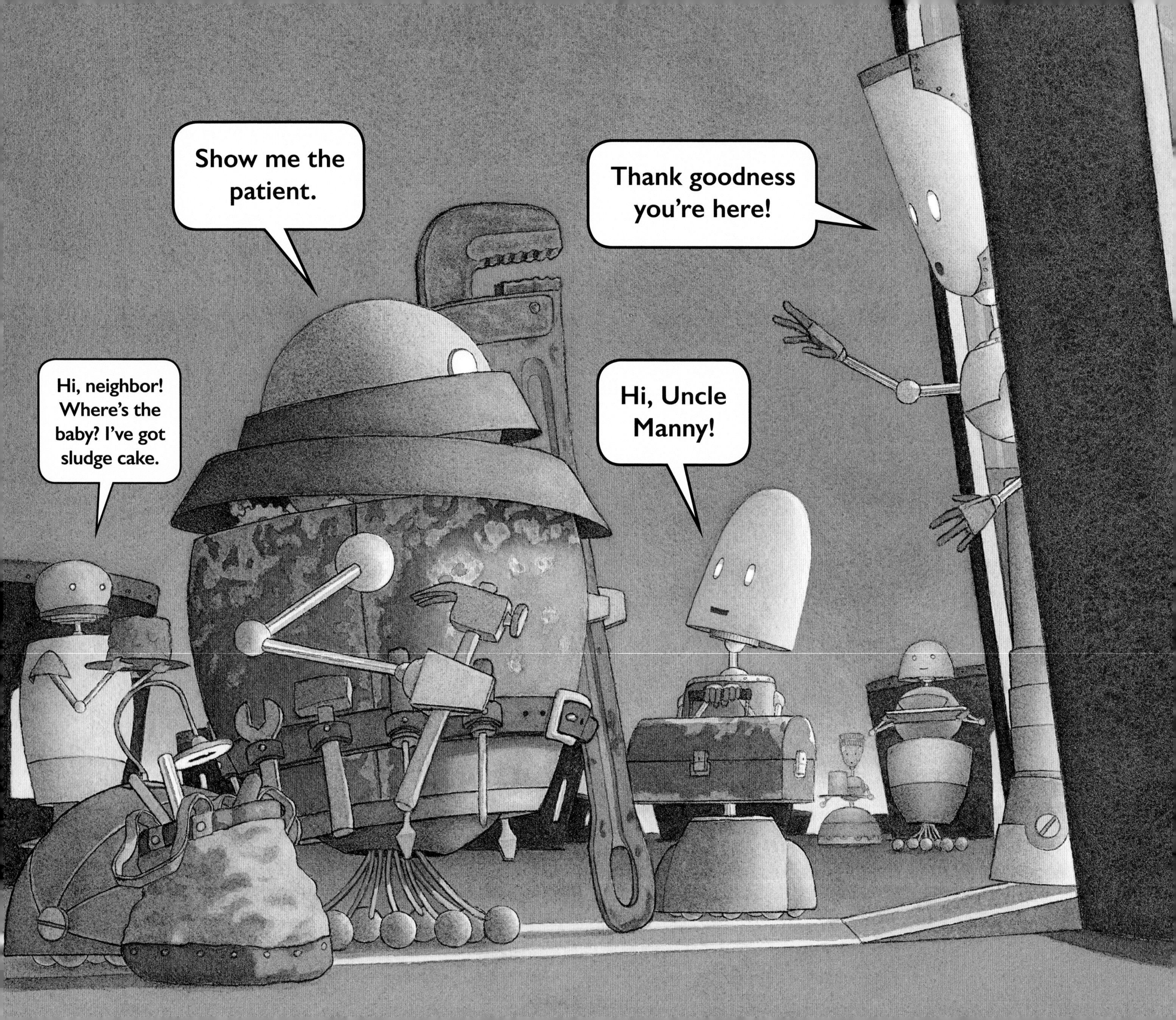
Hi, neighbor! Where's the baby? I've got sludge cake.
Show me the patient.
Hi, Uncle Manny!
Thank goodness you're here!

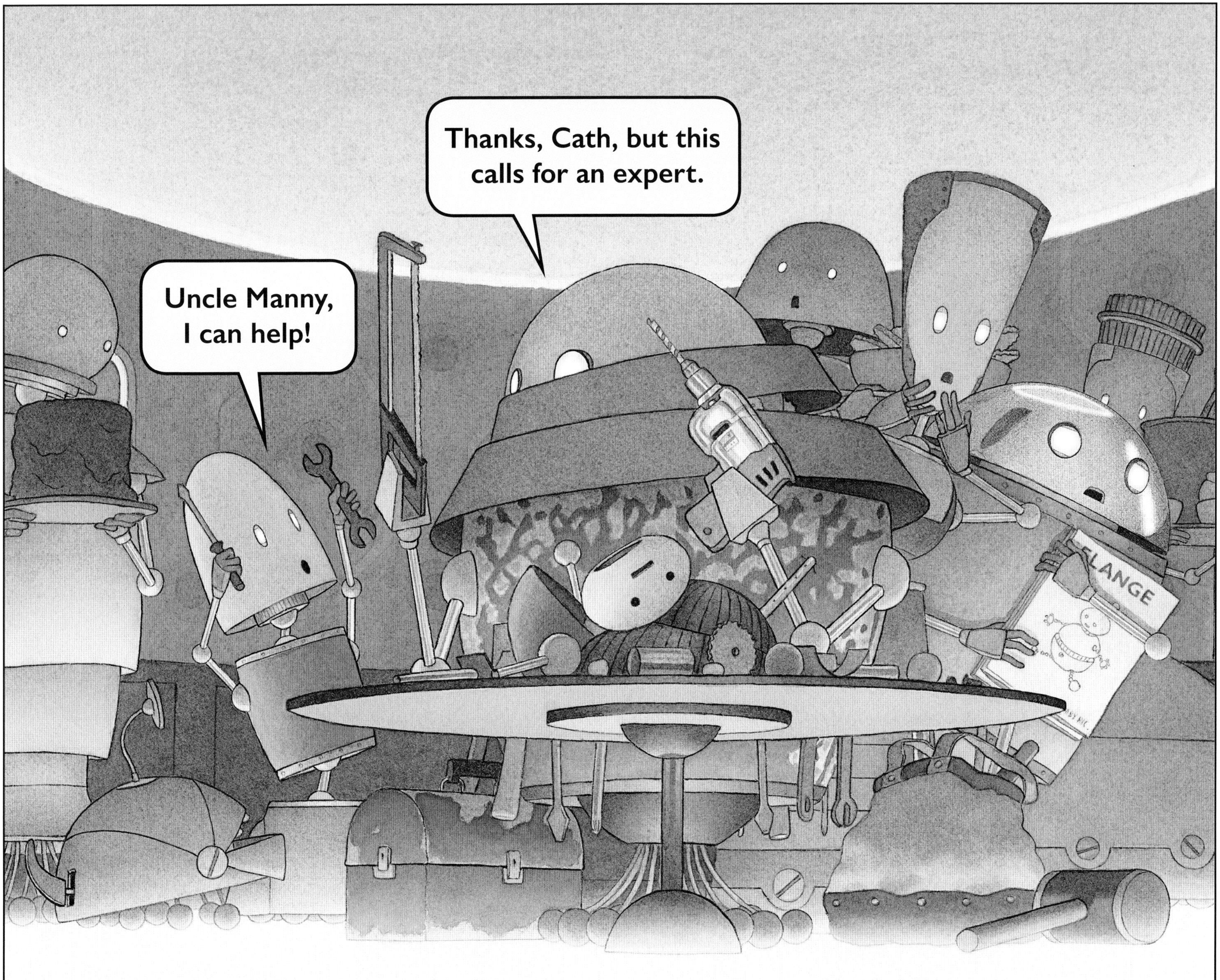
Uncle Manny, I can help!
Thanks, Cath, but this calls for an expert.

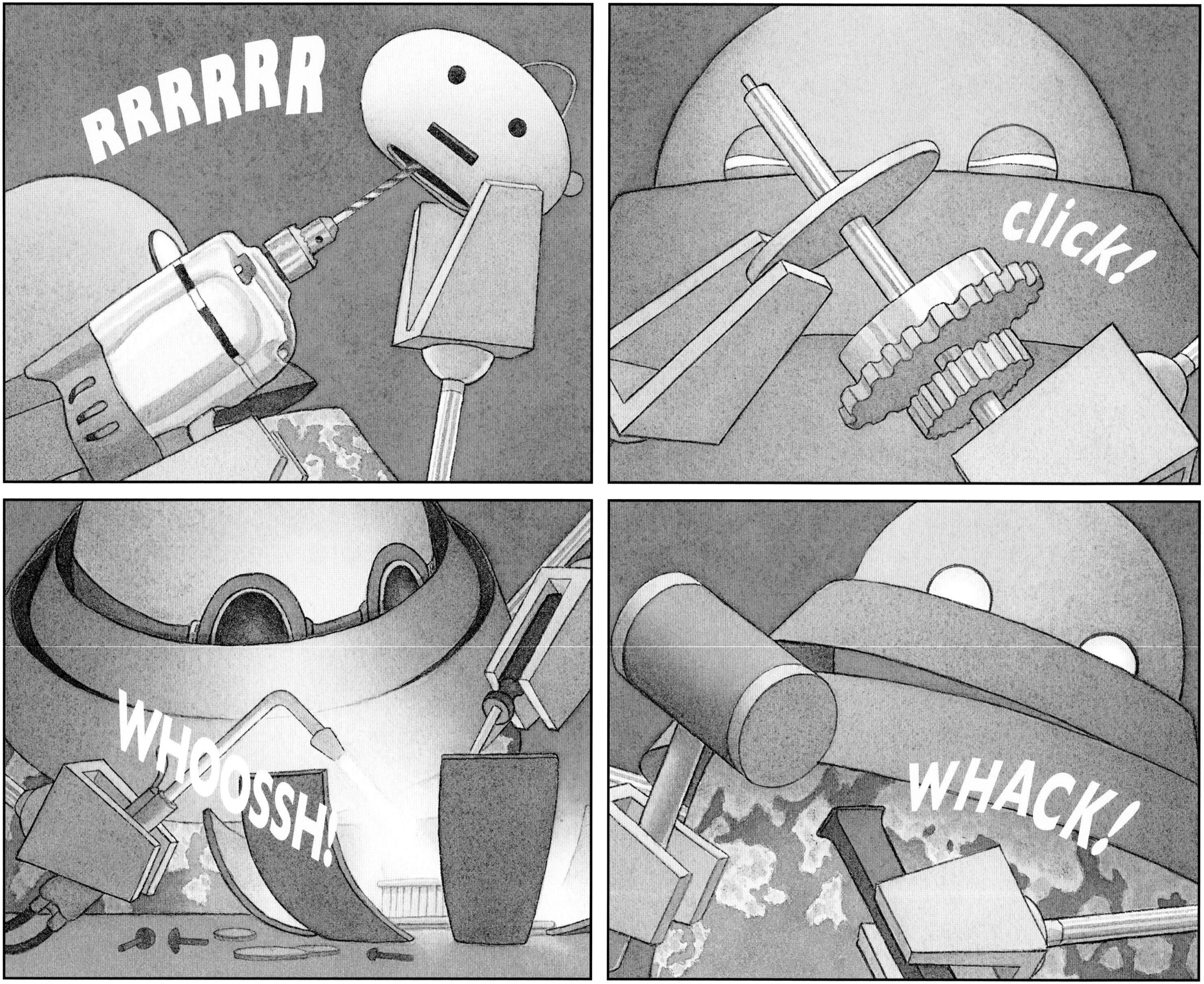
RRRRRR
click!
WHOOSSH!
WHACK!

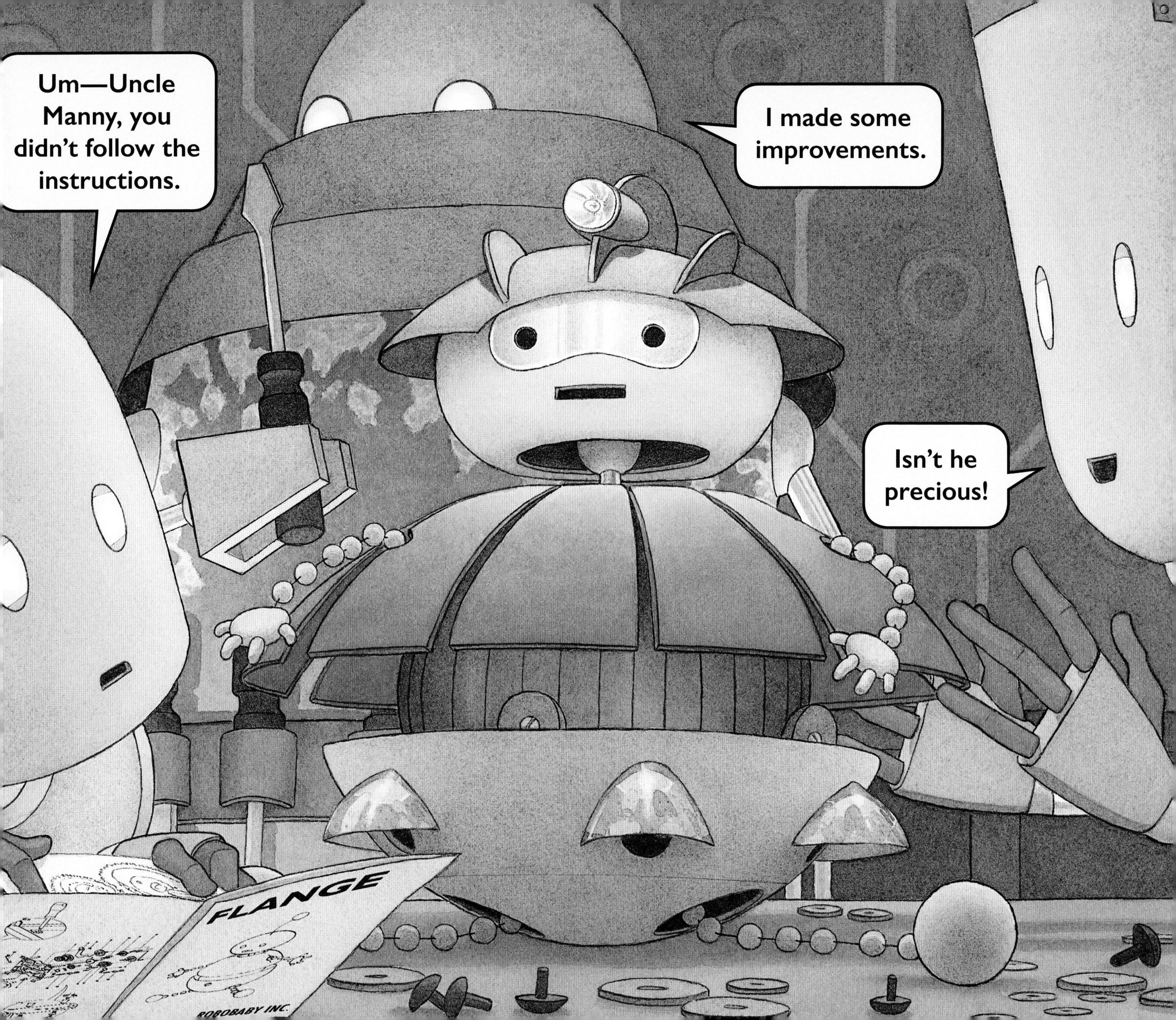
Um—Uncle Manny, you didn't follow the instructions.
I made some improvements.
Isn't he precious!
FLANGE
ROBOBABY INC.

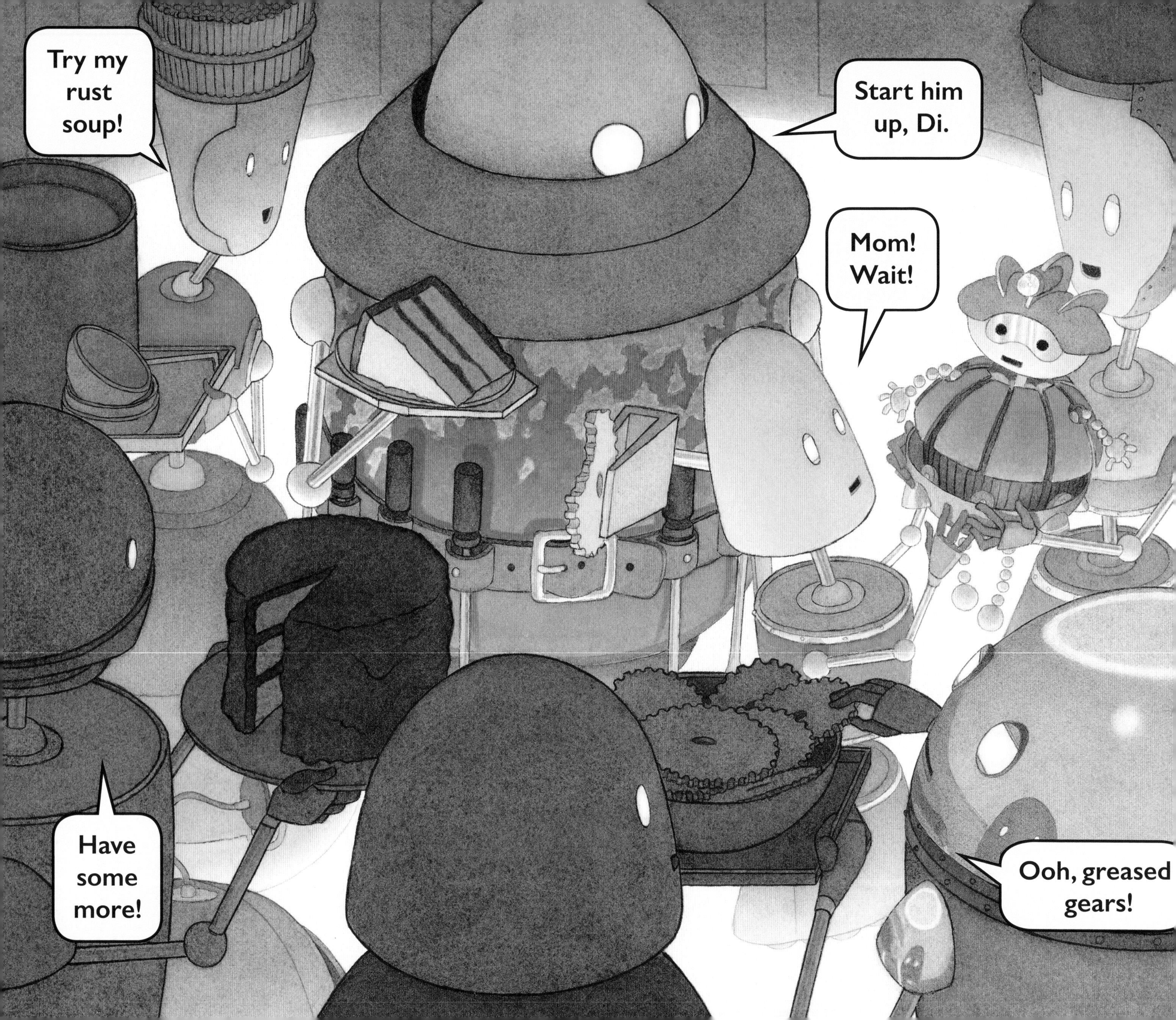
Try my rust soup!
Start him up, Di.
Mom! Wait!
Have some more!
Ooh, greased gears!

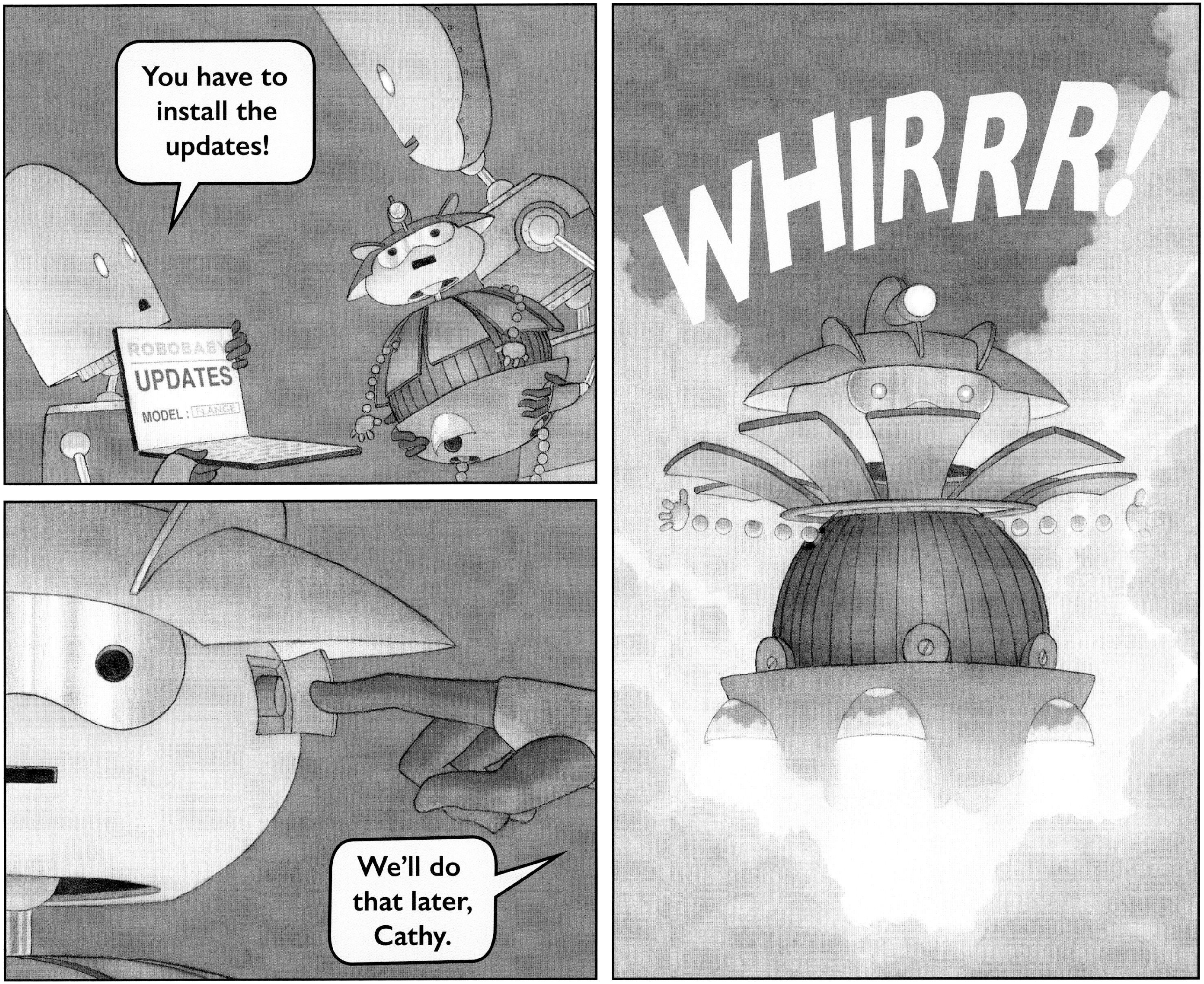
You have to install the updates!
ROBOBABY
UPDATES
MODEL : FLANGE
We'll do that later, Cathy.
WHIRRR!

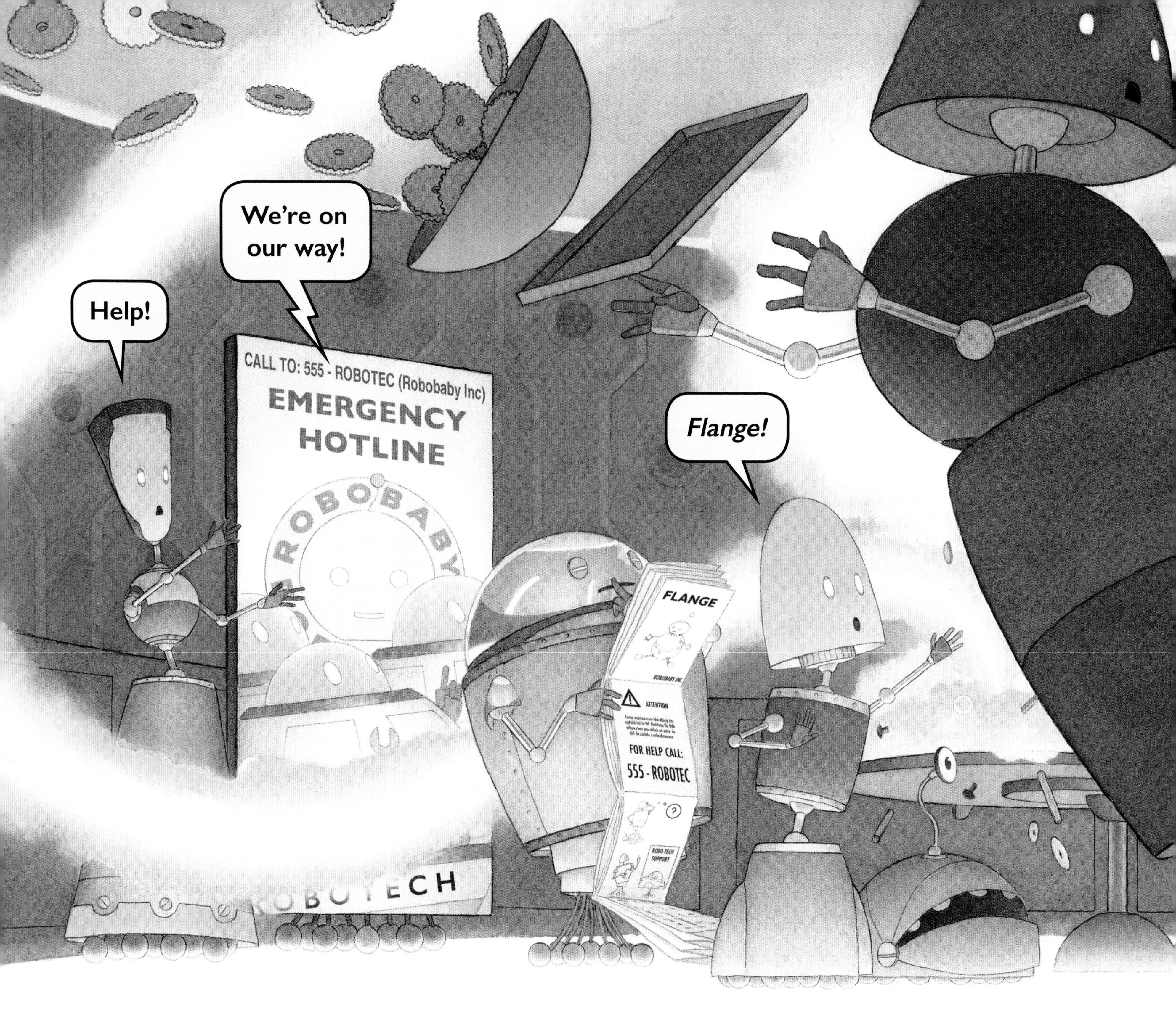
Help!
We're on our way!
CALL TO: 555 - ROBOTEC (Robobaby Inc)
EMERGENCY HOTLINE
ROBOBABY
ROBOTECH
Flange!
FLANGE
ROBOBABY INC
ATTENTION
FOR HELP CALL:
555 - ROBOTEC
ROBO-TECH SUPPORT

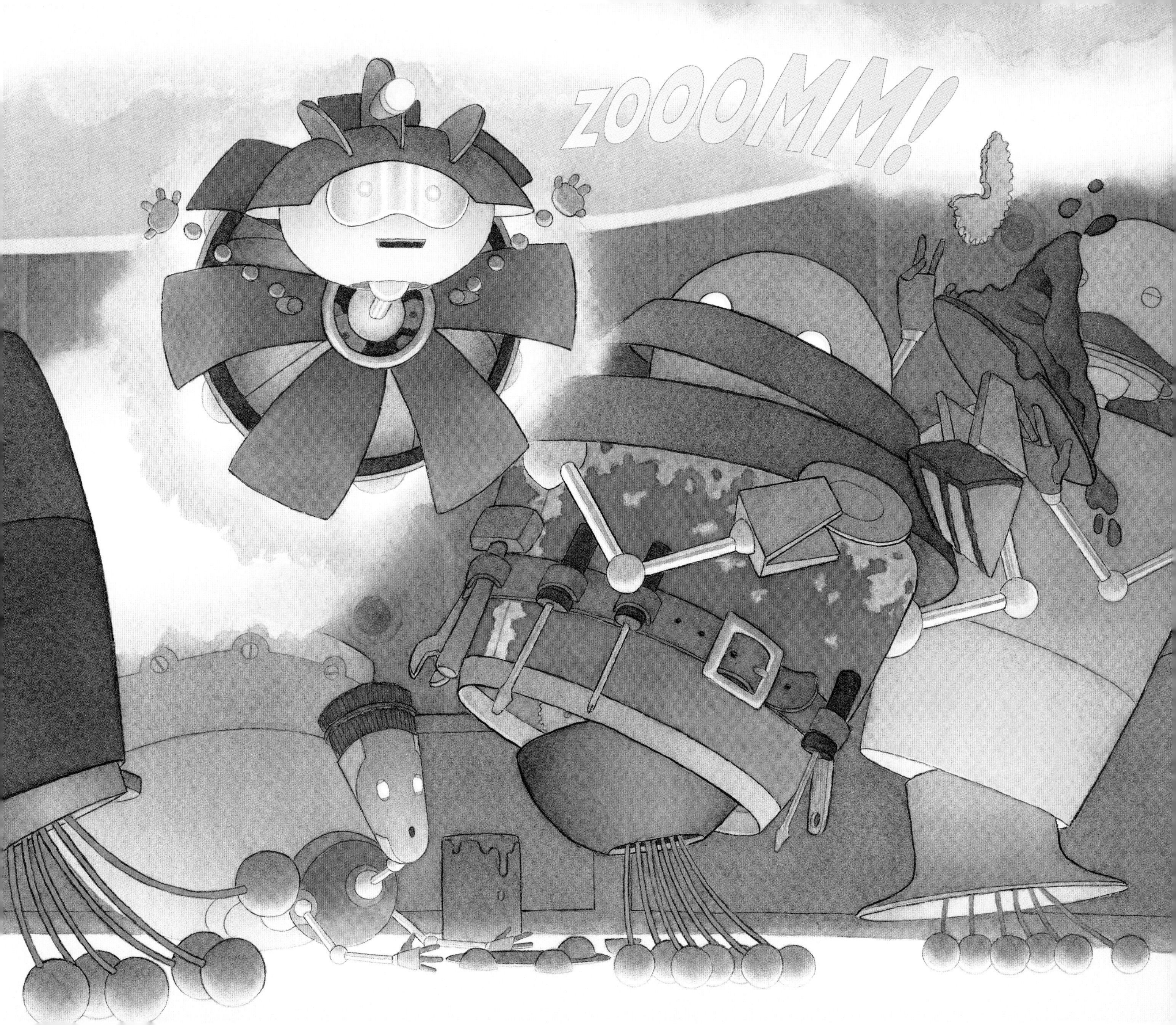
ZOOOMM!

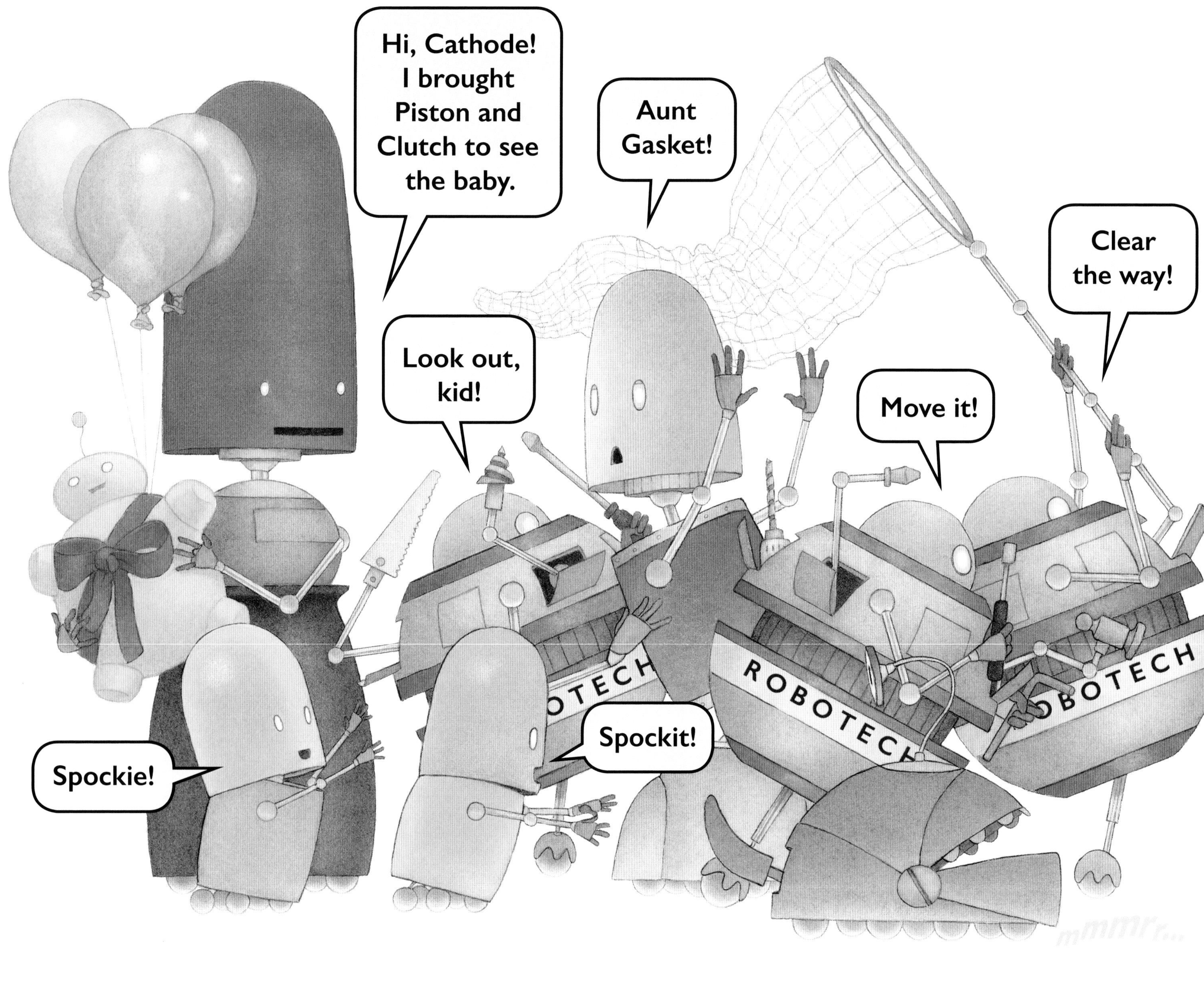
Hi, Cathode! I brought Piston and Clutch to see the baby.
Aunt Gasket!
Clear the way!
Look out, kid!
Move it!
ROBOTECH
ROBOTECH
ROBOTECH
Spockie!
Spockit!
mmmr...

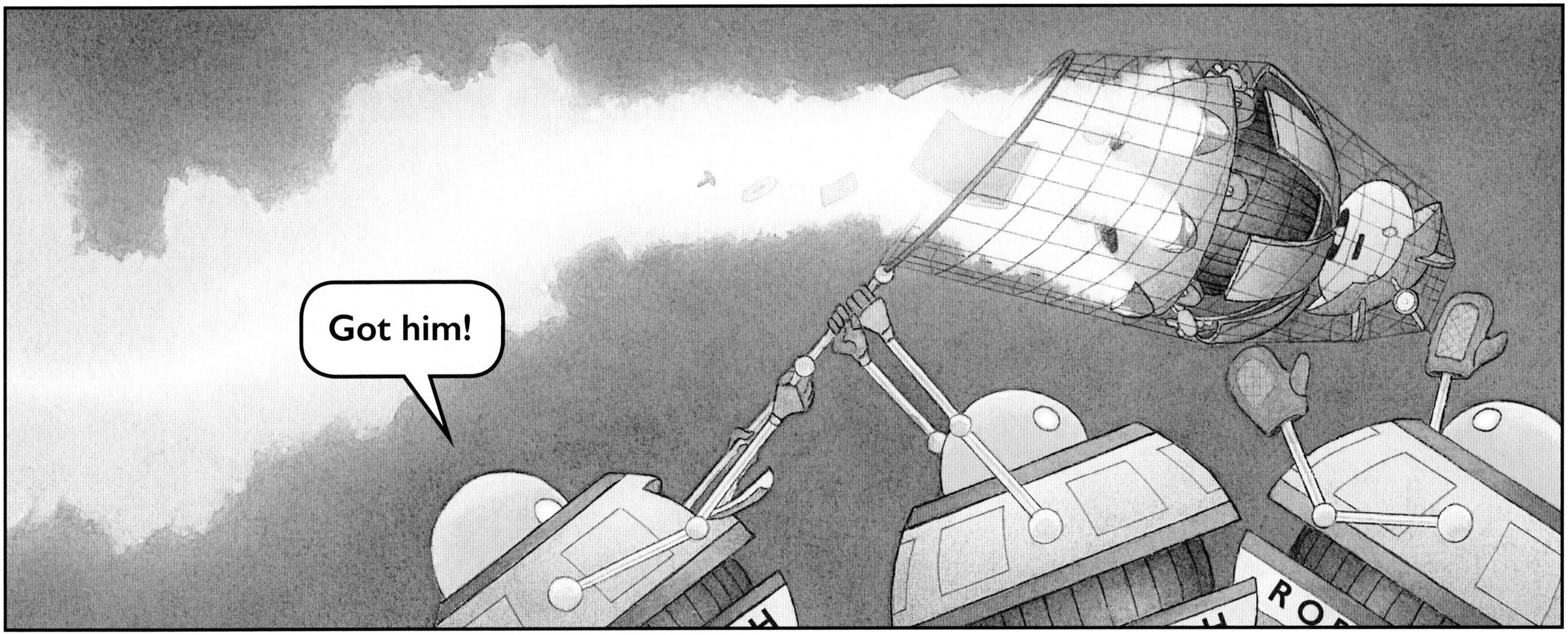
Got him!
ROBOTECH

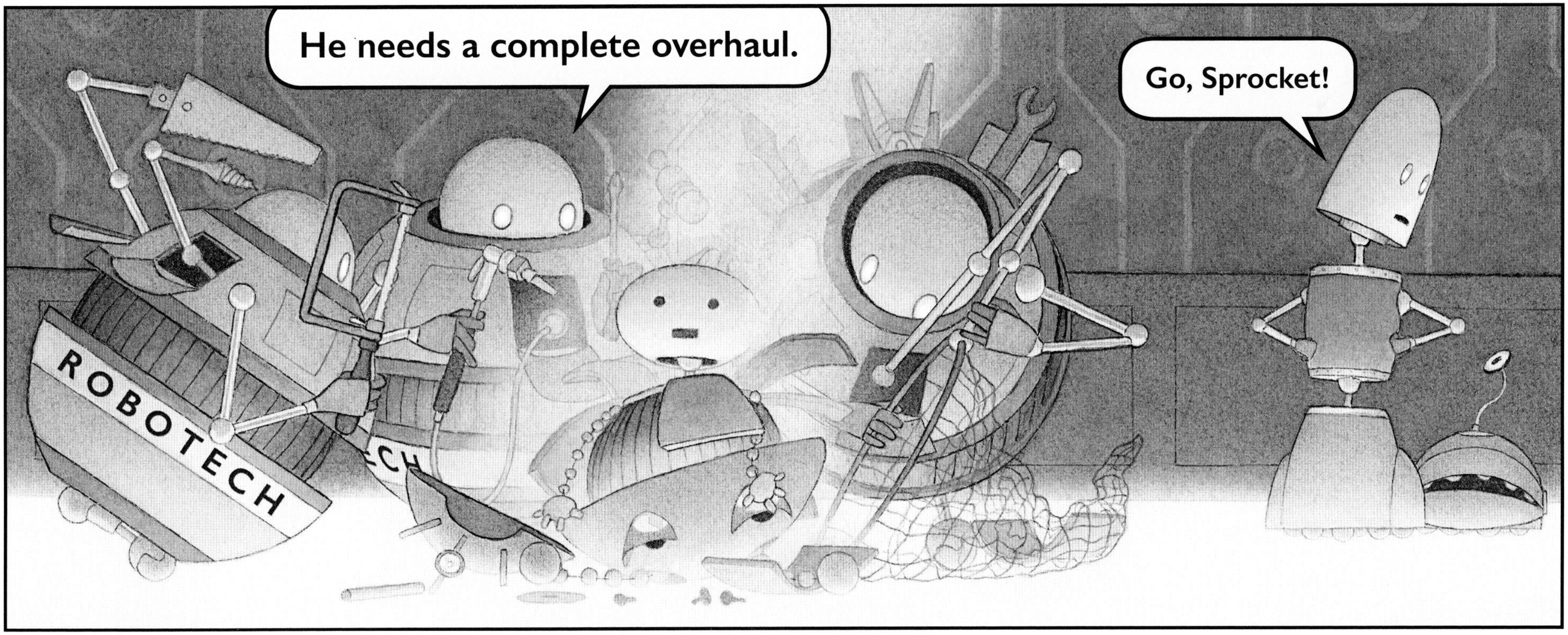
He needs a complete overhaul.
Go, Sprocket!
ROBOTECH

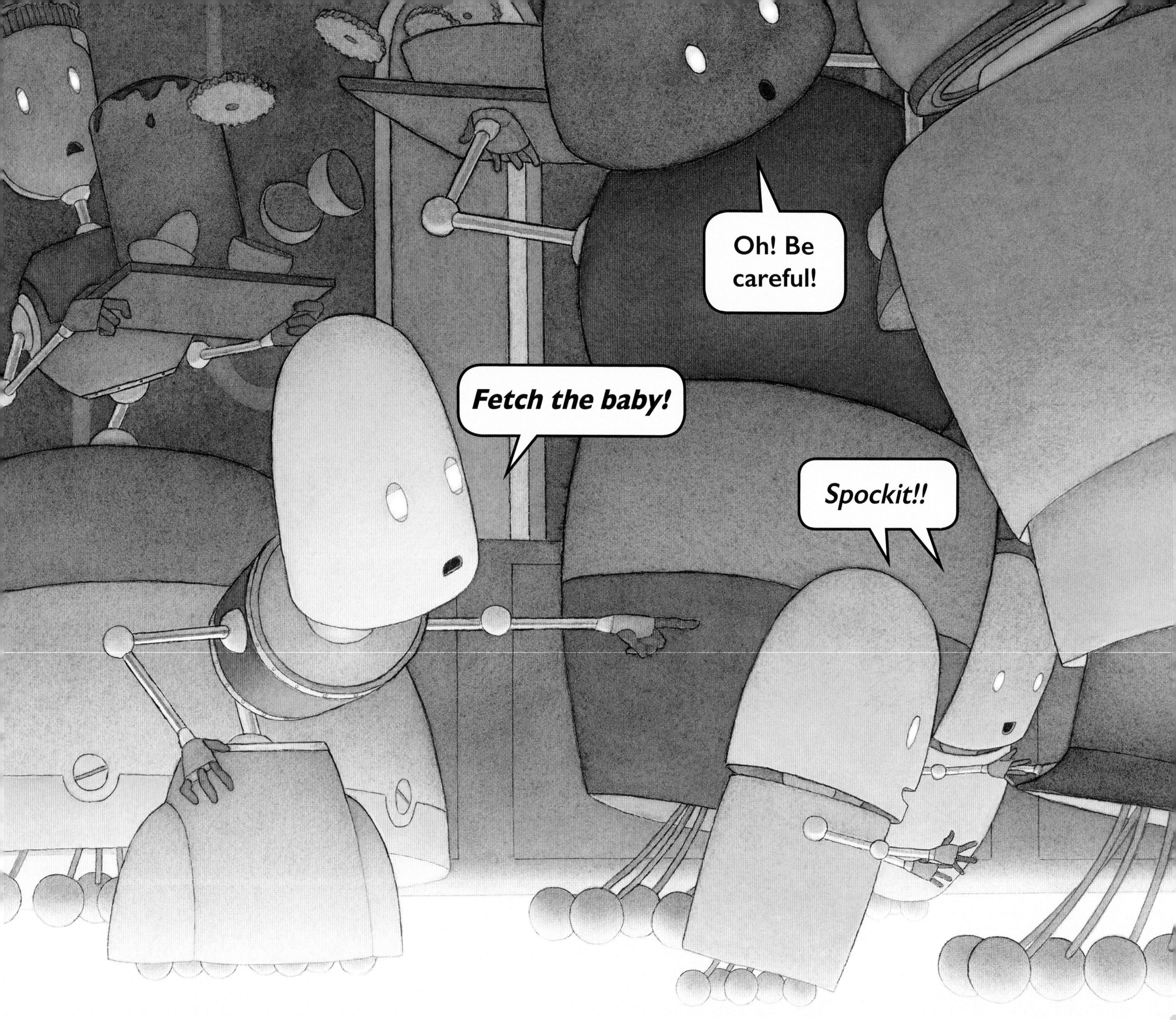
Oh! Be careful!
Fetch the baby!
Spockit!!

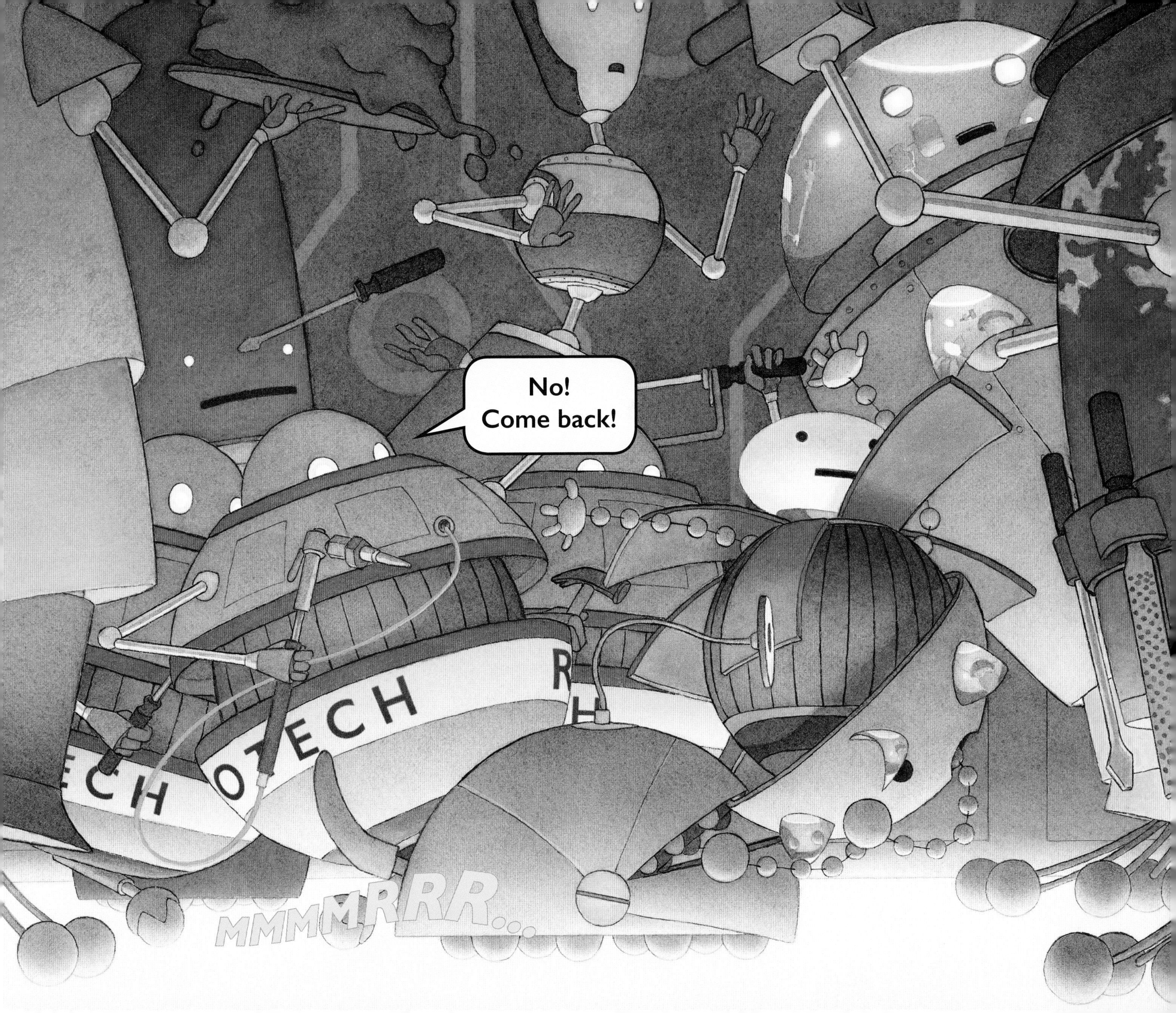
No!
Come back!
ECH OTECH
MMMMRRR...

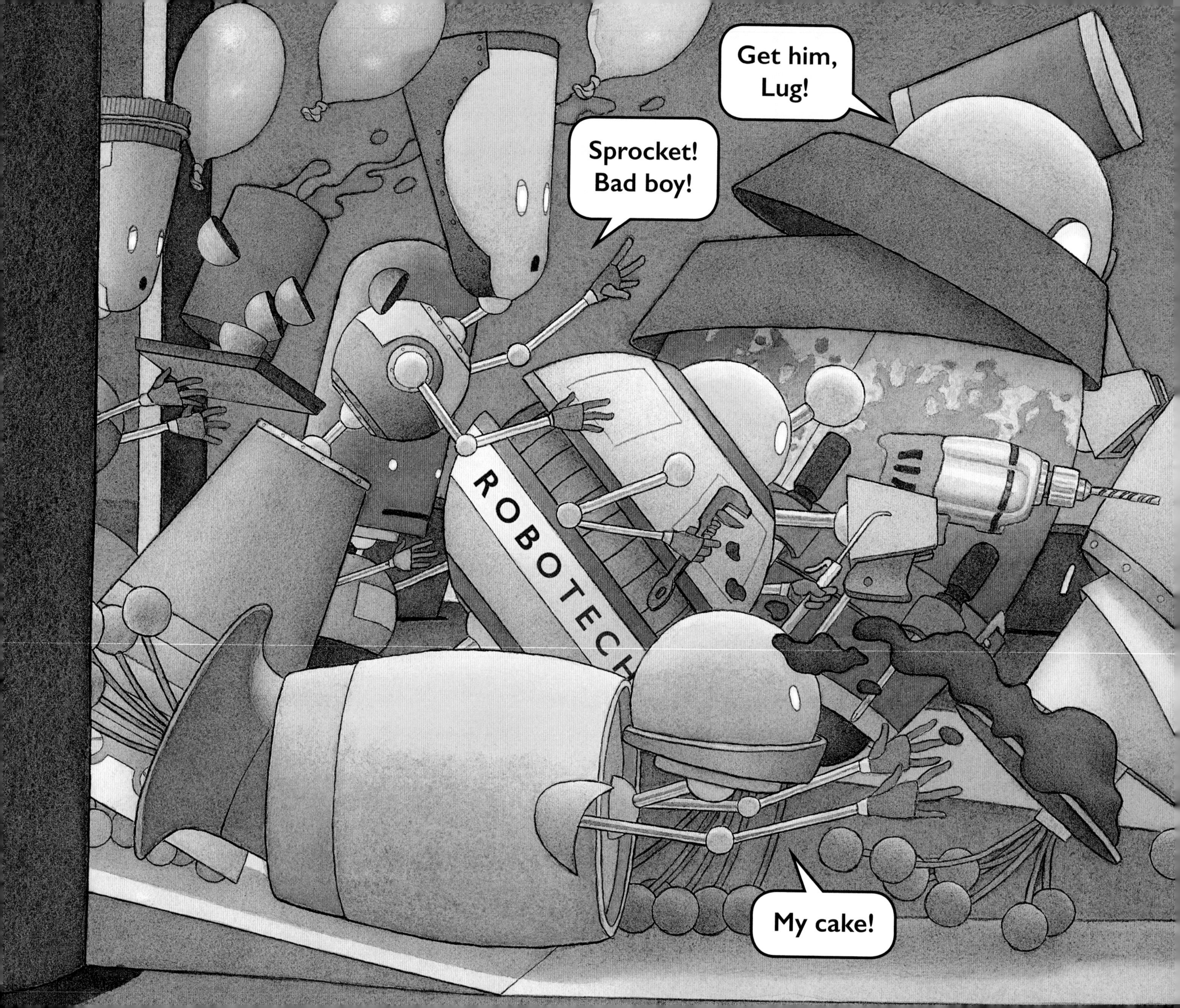
Sprocket! Bad boy!
Get him, Lug!
ROBOTECH
My cake!

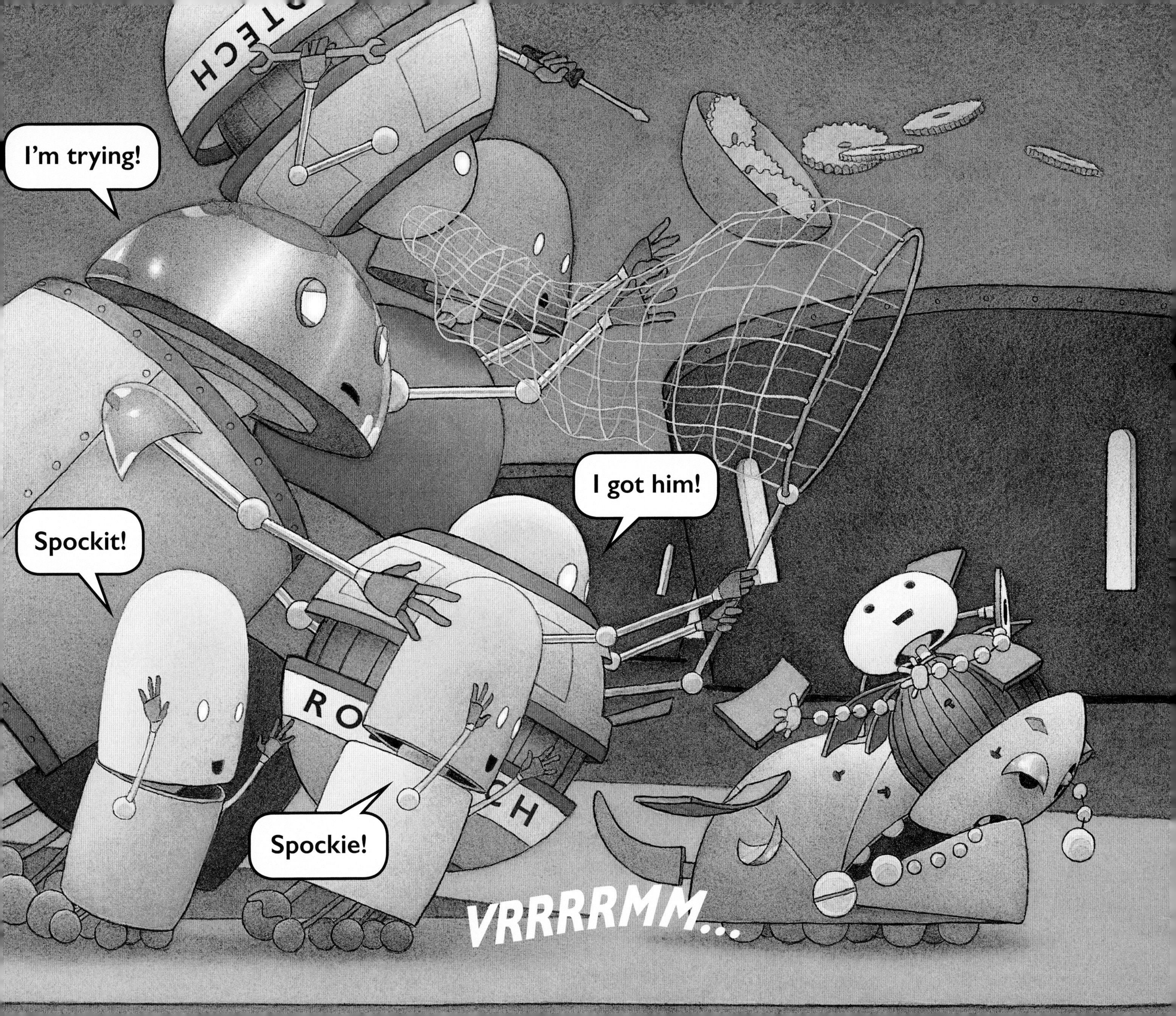
I'm trying!
I got him!
Spockit!
Spockie!
VRRRRRMM...

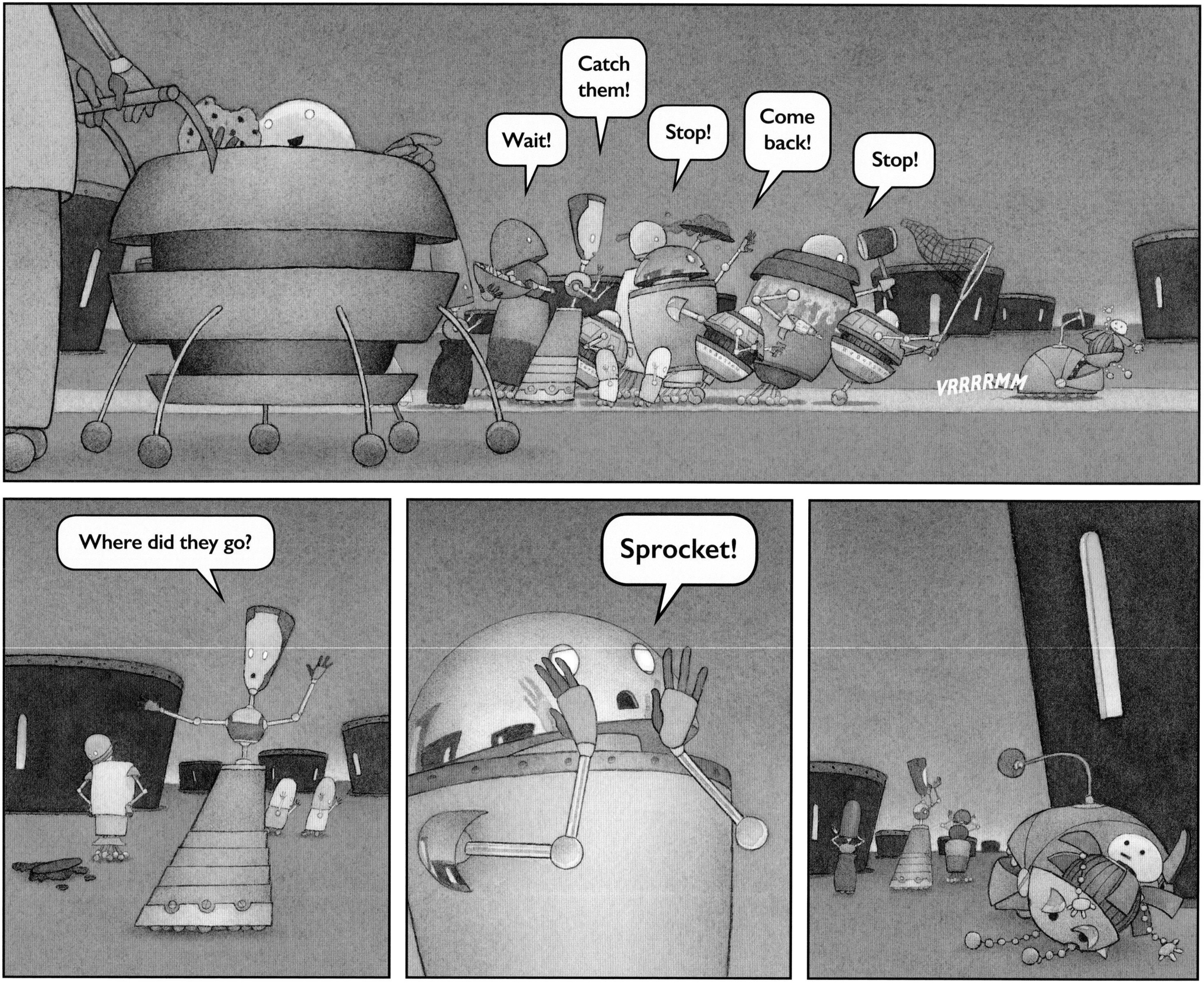
Wait!
Catch them!
Stop!
Come back!
Stop!
VRRRRMM
Where did they go?
Sprocket!

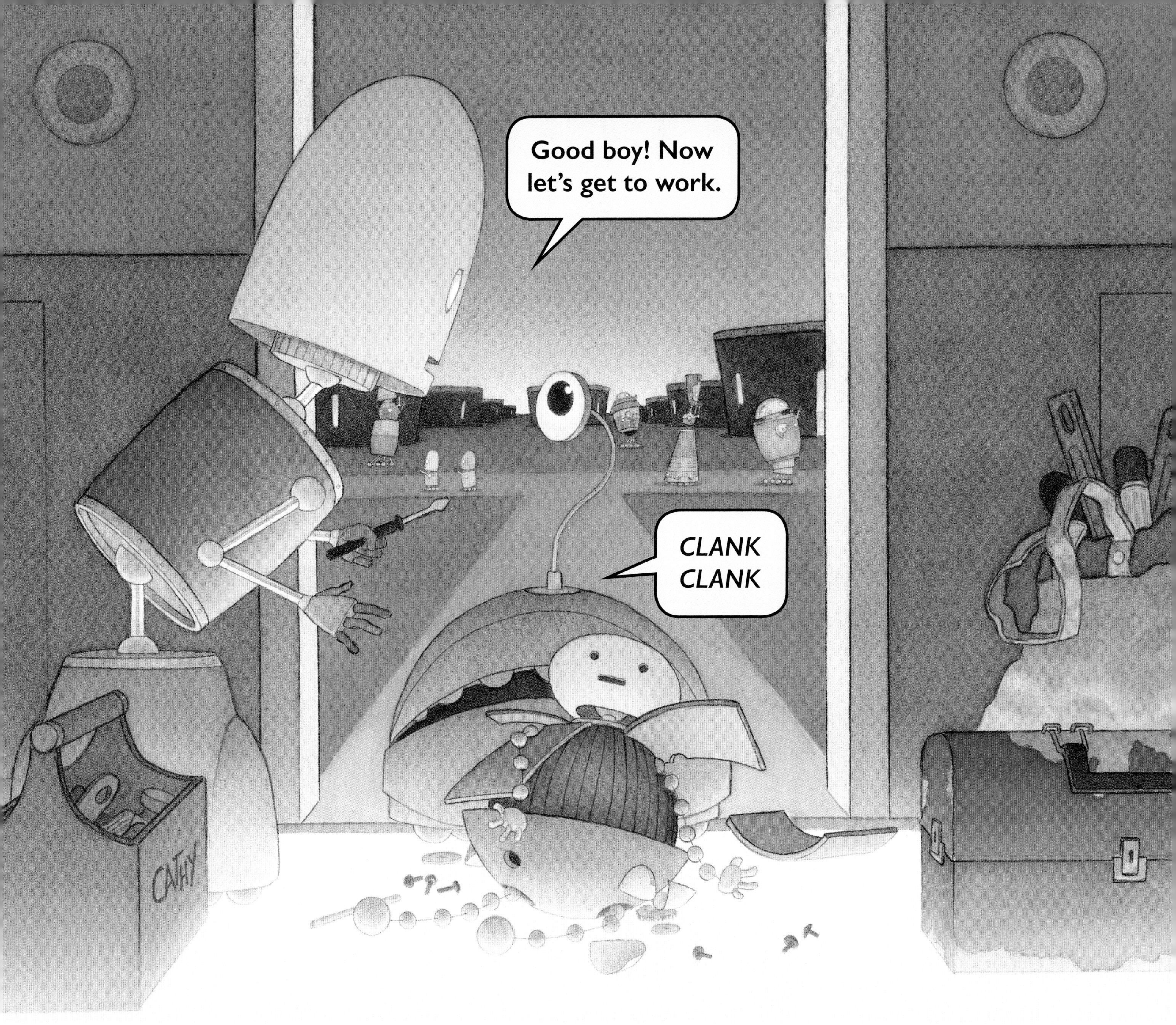
Good boy! Now let's get to work.
CLANK CLANK
CATHY

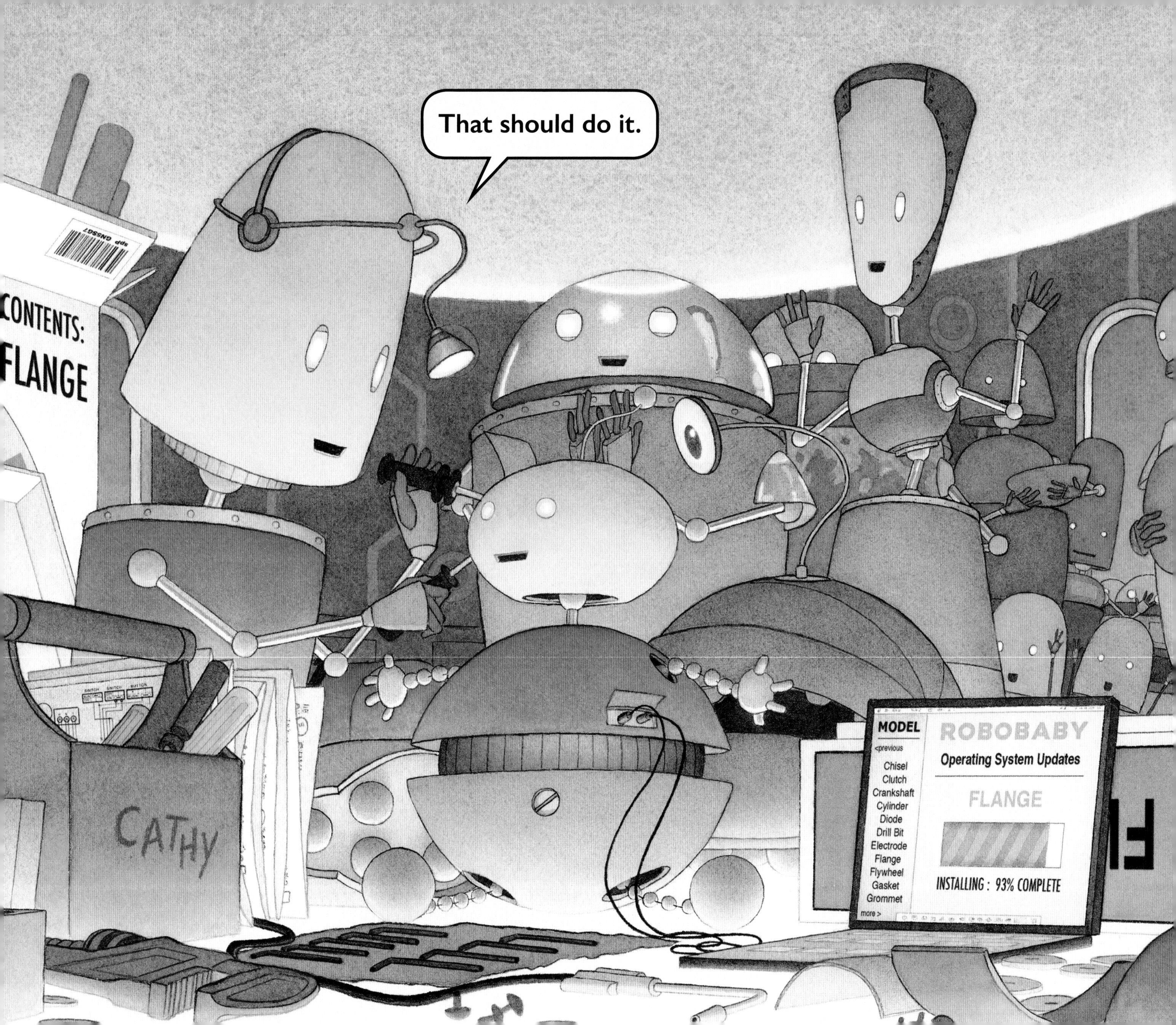
That should do it.
CONTENTS:
FLANGE
CATHY
MODEL
<previous
Chisel
Clutch
Crankshaft
Cylinder
Diode
Drill Bit
Electrode
Flange
Flywheel
Gasket
Grommet
more >
ROBOBABY
Operating System Updates
FLANGE
INSTALLING : 93% COMPLETE

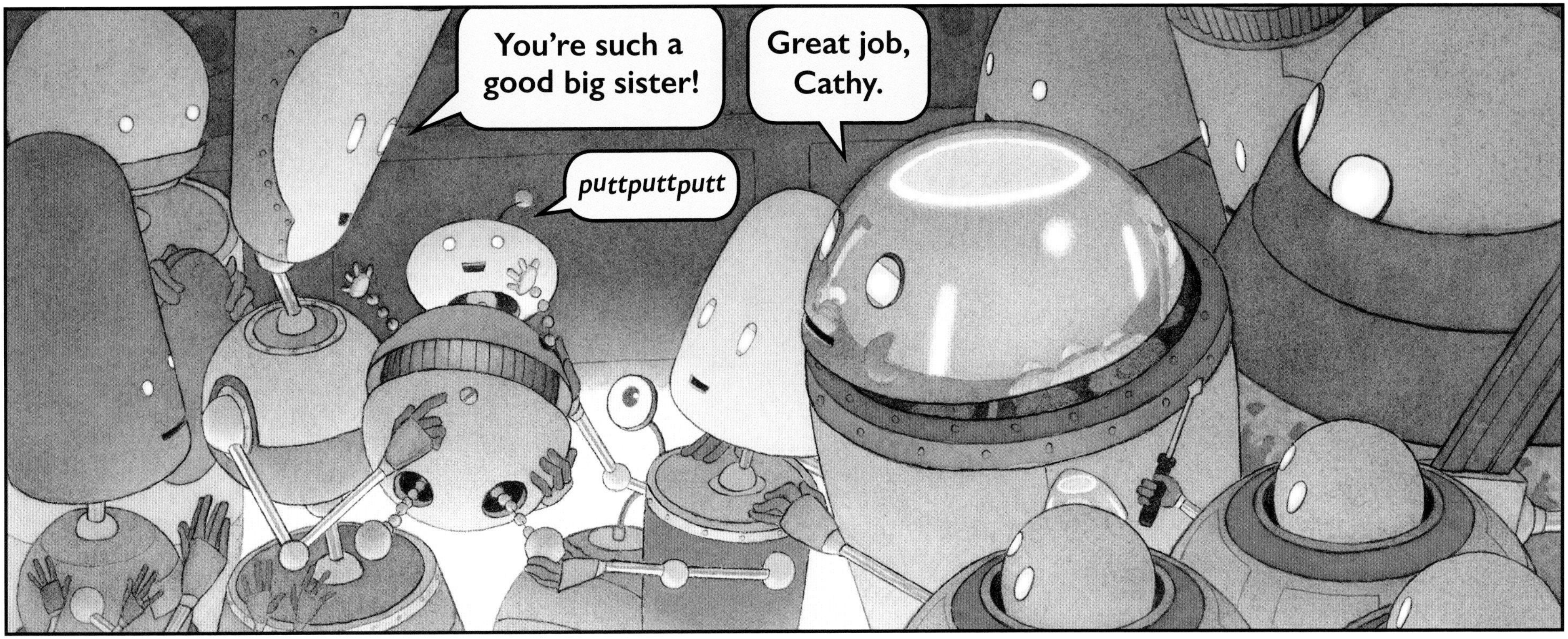
You're such a good big sister!
Great job, Cathy.
puttputtputt

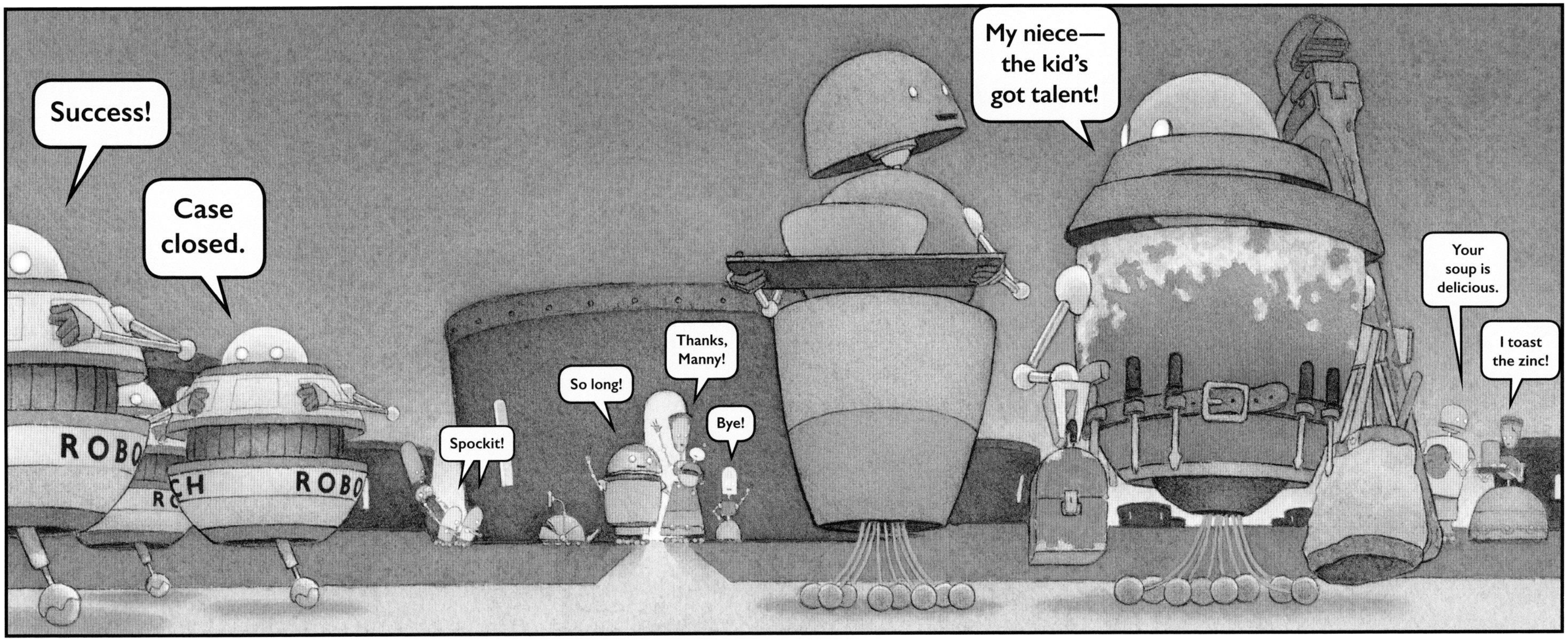
Success!
Case closed.
ROBO
RCH
ROBO
Spockit!
So long!
Thanks, Manny!
Bye!
My niece— the kid's got talent!
Your soup is delicious.
I toast the zinc!

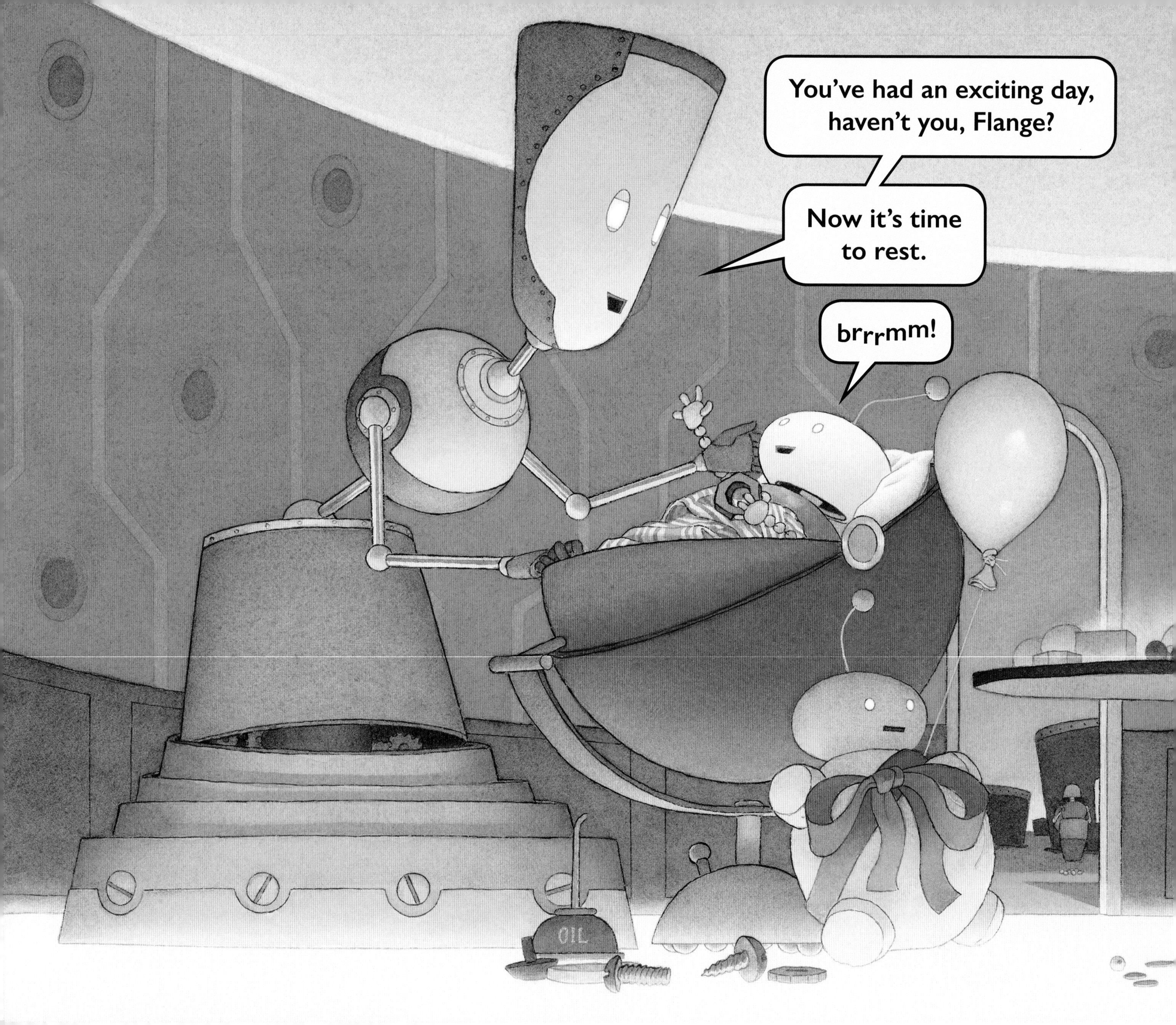
You've had an exciting day, haven't you, Flange?
Now it's time to rest.
brrrmm!

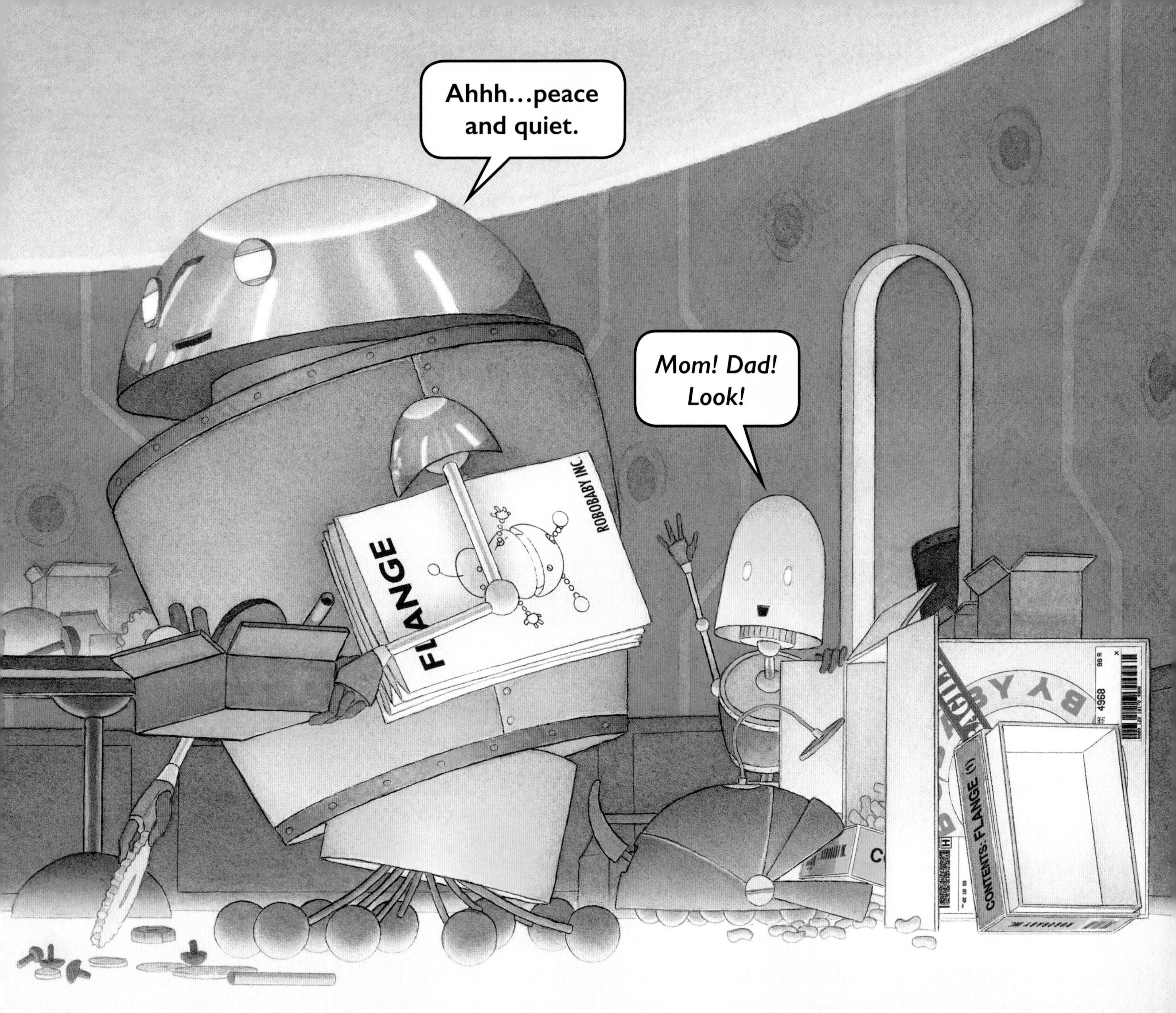
Ahhh…peace and quiet.
Mom! Dad! Look!
FLANGE
ROBOBABY INC.
CONTENTS: FLANGE (1)

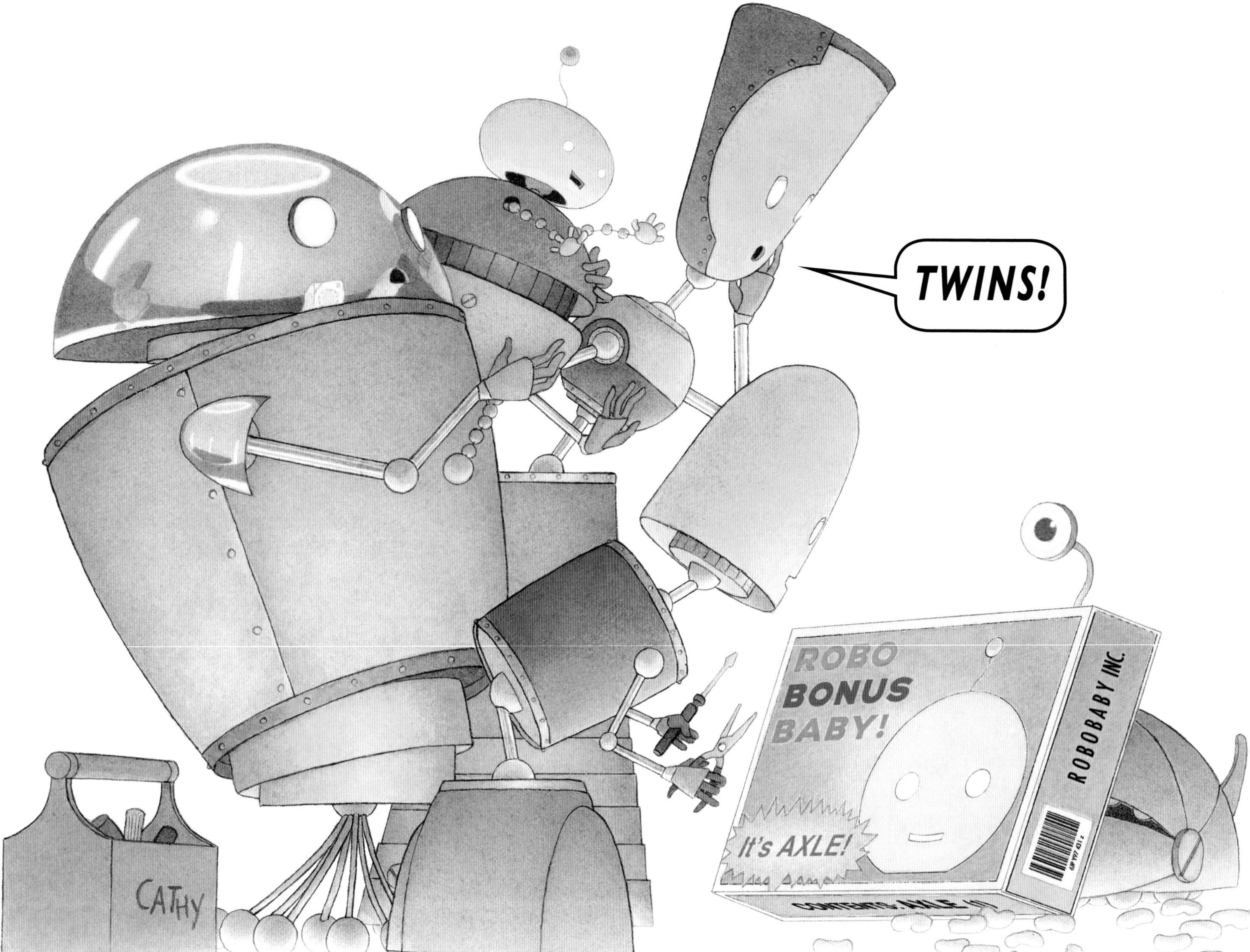
TWINS!
ROBO BONUS BABY!
It's AXLE!
ROBOBABY INC.
CONTENTS: AXLE (1)
CATHY